CHAIN THINKING

A Shep Harrington
SmallTown® Mystery

bancroft
press

Elliott Light

Published by Bancroft Press ("Books that Enlighten")
P.O. Box 65360, Baltimore, MD 21209
800-637-7377
410-764-1967 (fax)
bruceb@bancroftpress.com
www.bancroftpress.com

Also visit www.smalltownmysteries.com for more information

Cover and interior design by Tammy S. Grimes, Crescent Communications, www.tsgcrescent.com
Author photo by Sonya Light

ISBN 1-890862-21-5 (cloth)
Library of Congress Control Number: 2002116269
Printed in the United States of America
First Edition

"THE GREATNESS OF A NATION AND ITS
MORAL PROGRESS CAN BE JUDGED BY THE WAY
ITS ANIMALS ARE TREATED."

Mahatma Gandhi

CHAPTER
O   N   E

Except for the unusually cool weather, August 1 began like most of my mornings. By 7:00, I had showered, dressed, and finished breakfast, and was sitting on the porch nursing a second cup of coffee.

But then I noticed a cloud of dust rising above the trees that line the long driveway to my house. Moments later, a car sped out of the plume, its rear end fishtailing in the soft dirt. If I had known who was in the car and why, if I could have foreseen how allowing this visitor into my home was going to affect my life, I might have gone inside and refused to answer the door. Thinking back, I should have realized that only bad news travels this early and this fast.

As the car slid to a halt at the edge of the lawn, I bolted from my chair, stopping at the edge of the porch. For a long moment, no one emerged from the car, leaving me to muse that maybe it was driverless. But then a door swung open with a loud screech, and the driver, dressed in a burgundy cloak with an oversized hood, appeared. I had no doubt that my visitor was female. As she walked, soft fabric clung to her subtle curves, so much so that I wasn't sure if the cloak was all she was wearing. Her face was hidden behind a dark oval shadow, but I stared into the darkness anyway.

When she reached the porch, she asked, "You are a lawyer?" She spoke with an affectation that was sensual, almost arousing.

"Yes," I replied. "My name is Shep Harrington. Who are you looking for?"

A moment passed. I heard her sigh inside her cocoon. Then she said, "An attorney who went to prison."

Ouch! I had never considered my stay in prison a prerequisite to employment.

"That would be me," I said, "unless, of course, you're carrying a sickle."

I heard a quick laugh, but she didn't move. A moment later, she pushed back her hood. I don't think I flinched, but I'm not absolutely certain. Judging by her right side profile, she easily could have been mistaken for a model, perhaps in the middle of her career, but still physically attractive by any objective measure. But the left side of her face had been burned, damaging her eye and ear, and causing the corner of her mouth to turn downward. Despite the damage, something about her seemed familiar, if only remotely so.

She waited quietly for a moment. This, I sensed, was to allow me time to reflect on her severely disfigured face and to consider what it might be like to be in her situation. Finally, she asked, "You were expecting Snow White?"

The question had a practiced quality, originating not from some well-wallowed pool of self-pity, but from an inner strength. She was challenging me, trying to disarm me, using her misfortune to gain advantage. I admired her immediately, and raised the ante.

"I wasn't," I replied evenly, "but neither was I expecting the Phantom of the Opera." She glared at me, and I at her. Finally, her face brightened, and she laughed softly. "What can I do for you, Miss…?"

"What makes you think I'm not married?" Her eyes drilled into mine, then she laughed with such amusement that I couldn't help but laugh too. The mirth, however, was short-lived. "My name is Sydney Vail. I don't have much time. I don't have *any* time." Her voice quaked as she spoke. "I need your help."

"Are you in trouble?"

She shook her head. "I don't need your legal advice." She glanced at the car. "I work with animals that need help. Reilly Heartwood used to assist me sometimes. With Reilly dead, I didn't know where to go."

Reilly Heartwood was an older man who died eight months ago. I was the primary beneficiary of his estate and, apparently, his causes. "So you need money?"

"I have an animal that needs a safe place to stay for a few days."

"I don't know much about caring for sick animals," I said. "Surely you know other people who are far more qualified."

Sydney stared at me. "Kikora is not sick," she replied, her voice strident and demanding. "She is in danger. There is no one else. I have no choice. I need to go. You have to help me. Come with me."

"Wait a minute," I snapped. "Slow down."

"I don't have time for an interrogation," said Sydney. She looked at me impatiently, then offered a suggestion that sounded more like a directive. "Call Frieda. She'll vouch for me. But please hurry."

Frieda Hahn had been Reilly Heartwood's housekeeper before his death last Christmas. I went inside and called the house. Given the early hour, Frieda assumed that something bad had happened. "Nothing's wrong," I said. "I have a lady here named Sydney Vail. She's asking for my help, and she says you'll confirm that Reilly had helped her on other occasions."

Frieda was suddenly quiet. "She has a scar on her face?"

The question seemed understated given the extent of Sydney's injuries. "Yes."

"It's okay. Give her what she needs."

I hung up the phone. "Okay," I said to Sydney. "I'm game."

I followed her to the car and she opened the back door. When she turned around, I thought she was holding a baby. Only after a moment did I realize Kikora was a young chimpanzee. "She's asleep because I had to drug her to calm her down," said Sydney. "I have written instructions on what you need to do, how to feed her, and what to expect. I have some supplies in the trunk."

"I'm sorry," I said. "I can't do this. I don't know anything about chimps, you, or..."

"Do you want her to die?" Sydney looked at me, frustration and impatience in her eyes. "You're my only hope. You've got to trust me."

Kikora stirred and stared at me sleepily through large brown eyes. I was transfixed by the sadness and fear that I saw there. Sydney touched Kikora's cheek, then looked at me. "I will call you in a few days. I promise. This will all make sense." She saw my concern and forced a smile. "Taking care of Kikora isn't going to be that difficult. Until a few months ago, she lived with a family. She won't run away, so you don't have to put her on a leash. If she plays hard to get, she can't resist popcorn or chocolate. And despite what she's been through, she's in remarkably good spirits, so she doesn't have to be medicated unless something really upsets her." Sydney kissed me on the cheek, and got back into her car.

Kikora and I watched from the edge of the lawn as Sydney sped down the road, a cloud of dust eventually obscuring her car. I heard Kikora whimper, then felt her tighten her grip around my neck.

Life assumes a certain rhythm. The sun rises and sets, and in between we go about our affairs according to our whims and desires, oblivious to complex equations of cause and effect, and finding comfort in the illusion that we control our destiny. Sometimes, we arrive at a fork in the road and must choose one direction over another without knowing where either leads. Sometimes, the fork is chosen for us.

In just a few minutes that Monday morning, almost involuntarily, I had become a foster parent to a chimpanzee. Sydney said she would be back and all would make sense. Holding Kikora, I could only wonder.

CHAPTER
T W O

Kikora was awake but still groggy from the sedative Sydney had given her. I put her on the couch and sat next to her. She crawled onto my lap and I stroked her back. After a few moments, she turned her head and regarded me curiously through large brown eyes—eyes that were surprisingly human-like. "So," I said. "Here we are."

All I knew about chimpanzees I'd learned from watching television, and nothing I'd seen described how to care for a real chimp. I opened the bag Sydney had left and inventoried its contents. What Sydney had described as instructions were three typed pages of do's and don'ts with notes scrawled in the margins, a copy of a book entitled *All One Family,* a half-dozen diapers, a bag of apples, several boxes of popcorn, an assortment of brushes, and lots of ribbons. I glanced at the back cover of the book and then at Kikora. "We're cousins," I said, rubbing her back.

I located a towel and slipped it under Kikora, then went into the kitchen to clean the dishes. Twenty minutes later, a hooting Kikora was jumping on the couch. When I approached, she screeched and darted away.

After an hour of chasing, pleading, and baiting, I managed to trap Kikora in a windowless pantry. I called Frieda and told her I needed her to come out to the farm. I did my best to deflect her questions, then raised more by asking that Cecil and Harry Drake join her, with their tools.

A half hour later, I heard Frieda call for me. I answered from the dining room, and Frieda, Cecil, and Harry appeared. Carrie Toliver showed up an instant later. All four stood in a line, gawking at the mess that lay before them. Curtains were lying in heaps on the floor. The curtain rods had been pulled from the walls, leaving gaping holes in the plaster. By a single wire, a chandelier dangled awkwardly over the dining room table. The chairs were on their backs, partially covered by the tablecloth.

Cecil and Harry Drake are twins. I suspect they are in their sixties, but even they aren't sure when they were born. Other than their ages and a knack for working with their hands, they have little in common. Harry is tall, energetic, and engaging. Cecil is heavyset and aloof to the point of seeming dimwitted. I say "seeming" because Cecil is, in actuality, an expert carpenter and mechanic. His lights are on, I suspect, but the curtain is drawn.

Carrie Toliver is a small, almost frail woman with a sweet face and a head of cotton-white hair. She believes she's eighty-two, but she, too, isn't absolutely sure. Whatever her age, Carrie is deceptively perceptive, disarmingly witty, and remarkably strong-willed.

The reason for the uncertainty in their ages is that until last Christmas, they were the forgotten residents of the last poor farm operating in Virginia, the same farm I now call home. Cecil and Harry came to the farm as children after their parents died in a fire. Carrie is the only resident to have been born on the farm. A fourth resident, Jamie Wren, is a quiet, reclusive man who writes offbeat sayings for fortune cookies and greeting cards that appeal to city folk. No one knows when he first came to the farm or why.

It was a complicated set of circumstances that led me to the farm and sent the residents to live in Lyle, but the short version is that Reilly Heartwood, a country singer performing and recording under the stage name "C.C. Hollinger," bequeathed to me the farm, a mansion in town (named "Heartwood House" for obvious reasons), and an estate worth tens of millions of dollars. Before his funeral, I agreed to sell the farm to a developer and move the residents to the mansion in town. I intended to go back to live in my home outside Washington, D.C., but instead ended up in a local hospital with a gunshot wound.

By the time I recovered, I had no reason to leave Lyle and many reasons to stay. By chance, the deal for the poor farm fell through. Because I like my privacy, I moved to the poor farm. *Bottom line:* the four residents of the poor farm—Cecil, Harry, Carrie, and Jamie— live with Frieda Hahn, Reilly's former housekeeper, and Lora Jean Brady, a previously homeless teenager, at Reilly's amenity-laden mansion, while I live on a farm that sports a dungeon rumored to be inhabited by ghosts. Still, the farm is my home and the people who reside at Heartwood House are practically my family. Kikora could have done much worse than to end up here.

"What happened?" asked Cecil.

A crashing sound came from the kitchen. "Outside everybody, and I'll explain."

"Have you been drinking?" asked Frieda.

"Not yet," I said, "but hold the thought."

I managed to get everyone onto the porch and seated. "I need your help," I said.

"Will you please tell me what's happened here?" demanded Frieda.

"I'm getting to that," I replied, "but first I need you to understand that if you get involved, you may be committing a crime, at least technically. Even if you say no, you'll be a potential witness to a crime *I* may be committing. That means that I need you to be very careful not to talk to anyone about what I'm going to ask you."

"What kind of crime?" asked Cecil.

"Possession of stolen property," I said. "Perhaps some kind of accessory to a felony charge."

"I don't know," said Harry. "I've never committed a crime before."

"It sounds exciting," said Carrie.

"Stop with this chatter and get to the point," commanded Frieda.

"I need your help taking care of a baby chimp," I said.

Frieda stared at me knowingly. I was certain she knew the answer, but she asked the question anyway. "And where did you get this chimp?"

"From Sydney Vail," I responded.

Frieda was relentless. "And what in God's wisdom possessed you to agree to something so stupid?"

The eyes of Carrie, Cecil, and Harry focused on me, anticipating an answer. Another loud crash came from inside the house, but no one moved. "Because you told me to do what she asked?" I said, my answer sounding like a question.

Frieda glared at me. "I thought she was asking you for money. Reilly used to give her money. He'd never agree to take care of a monkey."

"Kikora is a chimpanzee," I said, "not a monkey."

No one spoke for a moment. Frieda folded her arms across her chest and gave me a how-could-you-be-that-stupid look. "All right," she said. "You have a chimpanzee. Why would that be a crime?"

"Because it's likely that Sydney stole the chimp," I replied. "Possession of stolen property is against the law. If we knowingly assist Sydney in getting away with theft, or even burglary, we could be considered accessories after the fact."

"If Sydney was involved, then I guess she stole it," said Frieda nodding. "And I guess Sydney told you that the chimp's life was in danger?"

"Yup."

"Every animal that Sydney helps is in danger of losing its life," said Frieda. "I don't know how Reilly could deal with a woman who goes around stealing animals for a living."

"My only other choice is to call the cops," I said, "and set the criminal justice system in motion. I've had my taste of that system, and I'm not inclined to sic it on anyone unless I'm certain they deserve it. I'm willing to take the risk of breaking the law for a few days until Sydney returns, but each one of you has to decide on your own."

"I think we should help Shep with his chimp," said Carrie. "Reilly would have wanted it that way."

"I'd like to help," said Harry.

Frieda shook her head. "As if I don't have enough work caring for the homeless. So what do you need?"

"Wait here," I said.

I went inside and opened the pantry door. Kikora was sitting in a pile of paper and cans. She had found a box of graham crackers and was busily trying to break through the plastic wrap that covered the package. I took a key from my pocket, slit the plastic, and offered her a cracker. Then I took her hand and walked her outside to meet the others.

"This is Kikora," I said.

"Oh my," said Carrie. "Look at her. She's just a baby."

"Who likes to swing and climb," I said. I gave Kikora another cracker, then handed the instruction sheets to Frieda. "Make a list of what we need from the instructions. I'll pay for it." I explained to Cecil and Harry that they needed to make the bunkhouse as chimp-proof as possible.

"Who's going to watch her at night?" asked Carrie. "She might not like being alone."

"I think she'll do fine in the bunkhouse," I said. I saw the empathy in Carrie's eyes. "But you can stay here if you'd like."

"We'll take turns," said Harry.

"We can install video cameras in the bunkhouse," said Cecil. "I saw a set of wireless cameras advertised on the Web for a few hundred bucks. Overnight shipping is extra."

"That's a lot of money," said Harry.

"It's not a lot of money," responded Cecil. His face lit up with a devilish smile. "Besides, it isn't my money. It's Shep's."

For the next hour, I straightened up the dining room while Cecil and Harry figured out what they needed to make a chimp-proof room in the bunkhouse. Frieda made her list while complaining about how she always had to clean up after other people's mistakes. Carrie brushed Kikora and talked to her. All seemed under control until Kikora decided that it was playtime again. For her next romp, she bolted outside and up a hundred-foot oak as if it had stairs. When she was a few feet from the top, she perched on a branch and hooted.

"Now what do we do?" asked Carrie.

I began to have my doubts about Kikora being easy to manage.

"Make popcorn," I said, "and hope she gets tired."

CHAPTER
T H R E E

The laws of entropy teach us that all matter is in a constant state of decay. I believe there are certain basic laws that govern how humans live their lives—laws that parallel the laws of entropy. According to one such parallel, whenever an event occurs to disrupt a human being's agenda, he or she will do whatever is possible to restore the agenda to the way it was before the disruption. Events are digested and handled this way so that the status quo can be preserved.

Of course, some events are so monumental that an agenda cannot survive. In my last life, I'd been a corporate attorney with a loving wife, but that life was nuked when I was sent to prison for a crime I didn't commit. I left prison without an agenda, only to be handed a new life by Reilly's death and the events that surrounded it.

For the past eight months, my work time has been split three ways: a small law practice, managing Reilly's estate work, and taking his place on a long list of charity boards and community service groups. I share office space in Lyle, Virginia with Robbie Owens, a local attorney and close friend. When I'm not at my office, I build and fix computers, watch the stars through a ten-inch telescope, and play the trumpet (the farm is a great place for horn blowing) and guitar. On weekends, I frequent the lesser-known blues bars in Georgetown hoping to get an opportunity to jam with professional musicians. I have a healthy social life, which means I don't have to be alone if I choose not to be.

Like most people, I must deal with an assortment of problems. Some, I created for myself, and others just decided to pay me a visit. I have some residual issues relating to a woman I shot in self-defense, and her husband's death. Most of the time, I cope with my collection of problems pretty well. Before Kikora arrived at the farm, my life had been orderly, and I was content. I was traveling enough to be stimulated, I was surrounded by people I care about and who care about me, and I had a nice place to retreat to whenever I wanted to be alone. Kikora's arrival brought a new set of issues that threatened to upset my orderly existence, an outcome I was determined to prevent.

The first day with Kikora was spent learning how to feed her, entertain her, and change her diapers. My first attempt at changing Kikora quickly convinced Frieda and Carrie that I was unprepared for foster parenthood, prompting them to take over the chimp-care duties. Harry and Cecil worked into the evening to convert the common area of the bunkhouse into Kikora's bedroom. All of the interior doors were screwed shut. Bars made of threaded pipe were anchored into the windows. Eyehooks were anchored into the ceiling rafters and ropes threaded through to give her a place to swing and exercise. Carrie took charge of entertaining Kikora, a task Carrie preferred to call "enrichment activities." At Carrie's suggestion, we introduced magazines, toys, and dolls to Kikora's room. With her care solidly in the hands of the residents, I was increasingly confident that Kikora wouldn't intrude on my time unless I wanted her to. I had, I thought, defeated the forces of entropy.

The video cameras arrived the next day. Harry and Cecil installed them, allowing us to watch and videotape Kikora whenever she was alone in the bunkhouse.

But then an odd thing happened. While in the barn, I bumped my head on an ancient harvester. When I came outside, Kikora saw the welt about my left eye. She was fascinated by it, even inspecting it with a certain solemnity. To my surprise, she drew the tips of her index fingers together and pointed at the wound.

I knew Kikora's behavior meant something, but wasn't certain what. Carrie observed what happened and recognized it for what it was.

"She signed the word 'hurt,'" said Carrie. "She spoke to you."

For over sixty years, Carrie had been nearly deaf. Twenty years ago, Reilly paid for hearing aids, but until then Carrie spoke infrequently and communicated using American Sign Language. My mother had insisted that I learn some ASL myself out of respect for Carrie. I actually enjoyed the idea of communicating in code, but I had forgotten most everything but the simplest words.

I awkwardly signed "yes" to Kikora and she signed back what I thought was the word "sad," then ran after a butterfly.

At first, I couldn't grasp the significance of this exchange. But as I watched her play, I couldn't help but think that something marvelous and profound had occurred. I'd had a conversation with a non-human animal, which had shown what I could only describe as empathy, and so I began to wonder. What else was she capable of? Where did she learn to sign?

Over the next few days, I suspended my usual routine and cancelled meetings for which my attendance wasn't mandatory. I spent this time observing Kikora and and working with Carrie on my signing so I could engage Kikora in communication. The problem wasn't Kikora, but my clumsy signing technique. With Carrie's help, Kikora recognized some of what I was signing to her (she responded to the signs for hug and tickle). But Kikora's patience with me was limited.

"I believe she thinks you're illiterate," offered Carrie.

With chimps, a college or law degree means nothing.

⌐∞⌐

On Friday, I had an appointment with a client in Reston, Virginia. I had finished a set of customer service agreements for a start-up company and had agreed to spend the day with the company's sales department explaining the legal implications of the contracts. After that, I planned to spend the evening in Georgetown listening to jazz and maybe sitting in for a session. Two hours into the discussion with my Reston client, I'd seen enough yawns and fluttering eyes to conclude that further discussion was futile. I agreed to send the head of sales a memo and adjourned the meeting.

I had no other commitments for the day and no compelling reason to return to Lyle. What I had were many questions about chimpanzees in general and Kikora in particular. I needed to talk to someone who could answer them. I had no idea who that person might be, but I knew someone who would.

Gary Fields is the Executive Director of the World Animal Federation, one of Reilly's favorite charities. I had met Gary shortly after Reilly's funeral. It was Gary who encouraged me to continue Reilly's charitable work, and who, inadvertently, helped me out of a funk brought on by Reilly's death and the events that followed.

"The man you want to talk to is Jerome Reinhardt," said Gary. "He's retired now, but he's been working with primates for fifty years. He's currently doing volunteer work at the National Zoo in Washington, D.C. The zoo exhibits orangutans and gorillas, but not chimps, so you won't be able to see any chimpanzees first-hand, but Jerome can answer any questions you have. I'll get a message to him and you can meet him at the zoo."

I headed down the toll road to McLean, and crossed the Chain Bridge into Washington, D.C. I parked on Macomb Street, then walked up Connecticut Avenue to the entrance of the zoological park.

I am ambivalent about zoos. On the one hand, animals are confined in their small cages, sometimes without others of their species. On the other hand, the animals are alive and offer most humans their only chance to observe them. The National Zoo offers decent habitats for some of its specimens, especially considering the zoo's limited size. Even so, I always leave zoos with a mixed sense of awe and sorrow. As I passed an enclosure, my first thought was that I'd entered a prison.

I was to meet Jerome Reinhardt at one o'clock, giving me an hour or so to wander around the park. I spent twenty minutes watching the big cats sleeping, hoping that one of them might do something other than yawn. I was momentarily excited when a white tiger stood up and stretched, but then he flopped over and resumed his snooze.

I noticed people hurrying toward the Great Ape House and decided to follow them. I couldn't understand what the excitement was about until I looked up. Some fifty feet from the ground was an orangutan gripping a cable with one hand, the rest of his body swinging precariously above the crowd. The cable was supported by a series of towers that linked two buildings a few hundred yards apart.

I was watching this performance when an elderly man approached me. "Shep Harrington?" I nodded and he offered his hand. "Jerome Reinhardt," he said. "Gary said you'd be here and gave me a brief description. He said you'd look like a lawyer, which you don't. I dare say I scared a half-dozen young men in suits before finding you."

"My clients are high tech," I said. "Sometimes I press my blue jeans, sometimes I don't. They don't like it if I overdress. Anyway, I appreciate your taking the time to find me and talk to me."

Jerome was a small man, with narrow shoulders, a long thin nose, and an uneven gray beard. His height was hard to judge because of a severely curved spine, but I doubt he was ever over five-six. Despite his withered appearance, his eyes were bright and full of fire.

He pointed to the orangutan swinging above us. "That's Clyde. Smart as a whip."

"What's he doing?" I asked.

"The cable he's dangling from is part of the Orangutan Transit System," answered Jerome in a practiced speech. "The system comprises eight towers with two parallel cables strung between them that allow orangutans to traverse the span between the Great Ape House, where they sleep, and the Think Tank, where they go to school."

"School?"

"We teach the orangutans a symbolic language," he replied, "using computers." We watched Clyde for a moment. "Gary said you wanted to know something about chimpanzees."

"I have a lot of questions," I replied, "but I'm curious about our attempts to communicate with them. I know some have been taught American Sign Language. I was wondering if they know what they're saying or just mimic their human teachers."

Jerome rolled his eyes. "Of course they know," he said, grabbing me by the arm. "I'm not supposed to say that. I'm supposed to let visitors make up their own minds. Clearly, any visitor that thinks otherwise is an idiot." He laughed again. "I don't have to be objective any more, Shep. I'm retired. Walk with me and I'll give you a brief history lesson."

Jerome walked in short, quick steps. It took me a moment to adjust to his gait.

"We first attempted to communicate with primates in the 1930s and '40s," he said. "I was involved in an experiment with chimpanzees. We wanted to teach them a limited vocabulary so they could talk to us. It became clear they could understand what we said, but, of course, they never spoke. Mind you, it was our ignorance, not theirs, that kept us from communicating. It took twenty-five years before Allen and Beatrix Gardner suggested that their problem was the inability to vocalize, not communicate. The Gardners decided to teach American Sign Language to a chimpanzee named Washoe, who's now in a sanctuary. She's learned nearly three hundred signs. She's also taught her adopted son, Loulis, to sign. She's been observed forming his fingers into signs. The chimps construct their own phrases for things and use them to express notions like 'Gimme tickle' or 'You me go out.' It's amazing what our relatives can do."

"But what are they thinking?" I asked.

The question brought a bemused smirk to my mentor's face. "Your question assumes that chimps are thinking, which of course I believe to be the case. A few of my colleagues would fuss about your conclusion, but they're dunces of the first order. As to what a chimp might be thinking, well, that's not something I can answer. You should ask the chimp." He chuckled gleefully at his last statement, and I couldn't help laughing myself.

We stopped at an outdoor exhibit occupied by a half dozen gorillas. "You haven't told me why you're asking about chimps," said Jerome. He held up his hand to keep me from responding. "That's okay, but what you may not appreciate is that by inquiring at all, you have called attention to yourself. For all of the people associated with chimps, only a very well-known group of researchers actually studies them, and only a small number of labs in this country use them as test subjects. The scientists who have intimate knowledge of primate cognition and behavior know each other and know, through a very efficient grapevine, what's happening in each other's patch. I know, for example, that Celia Stone, a research scientist at Doring Medical Incorporated in Virginia, was murdered a few weeks ago. I also heard a rumor that a chimp was stolen from her house. I'm sure DMI and the authorities are looking for it. You show up here, an attorney, and want to know something about chimpanzees. You don't have to be a scientist to put two and two together. I'm no threat to you, but you should be careful who you confide in." He looked at me sternly. "Are you following what I'm saying?"

"Yes," I said, trying to deal with a new possibility—that Sydney Vail was involved in murder as well as theft.

"If you have the chimp, or if you have a client who does, it is only a matter of time until you're exposed," continued Jerome.

I thought for a moment. "You said something about a chimp at a sanctuary. Maybe I could contact someone…"

Jerome raised both hands and waved them at me in disgust. "No, no, no," he said. "A stolen chimp is not going to be accepted anywhere. Even if you found someone willing to take the legal risk, there are hundreds of chimps that need homes already." He groaned. "I could talk to you about primates for days, weeks even. Why don't you tell me what brought you here?"

I told him about Kikora signing to me.

"You're very perceptive," he said approvingly. "The voluntary initiation of communication is stunning enough. That she exhibited empathy is fascinating, but not surprising. Empathy requires the ability to stand in the shoes of another entity, something that human children lack until age three or four. It is evidence that Kikora not only has a mind, but is aware that you have one, too."

"I guess she doesn't know that I'm a lawyer," I quipped.

Jerome laughed softly. "I wish I'd thought to say that."

"I tried, but she wouldn't sign to me again," I said. "I want to talk to her. I don't know why exactly." I shook my head. "Maybe I'm seeking an intelligent life form here on earth."

"We can talk about futility at another time," said Jerome with a chuckle. "Your chimp needs to trust you. Conversing with a stranger, certainly after what this creature has gone through, is a leap of faith for her. After all, someone taught her to sign and then gave her up." Jerome grimaced. "I have a guess who that might be," he said disparagingly. "Anyway, her not signing to you is a defense mechanism, which itself is more evidence of innate intelligence."

Jerome looked at his watch. "I must go," he said, "but I'll try to help you if I can." I expected him to leave, but he continued to watch the gorillas below us. "I don't approve of using primates as medical test subjects," he said finally. "For one thing, they aren't perfect models of humans. A lot of chimps were bred for use in AIDS testing. The research community didn't know, or want to believe, that chimps don't get AIDS, so they kept trying to infect chimps with the virus. Of course, some untold number of chimps died as a result of forcing ever-higher doses of the virus into their systems."

Jerome seemed to struggle with his thoughts. "Do you know that we used to steal baby chimps from their mothers? The mothers were often killed, and the babies brought here to be infected with some disease or trained to perform for the entertainment of their human captors. I guess we've gotten more moral because now we use animals that are born in captivity." He shook his head. "Then again, the population of wild chimps continues to decline as we shoot them for their meat and harvest their habitat. No one actually knows how many are left in the wild, but it isn't likely to be more than a few hundred thousand. Researchers estimate that the population will decline by eighty percent in the next thirty years—just two generations of chimps." Jerome looked at me. "We have driven a species close to the edge of extinction for the benefit of an overpopulated human herd. It's indefensible." He tried to say more, but looked away instead.

"Some good must come from the medical studies," I said confidently.

Jerome looked at me in disbelief. "Good? I suspect that, on some level, an ignorant person might find good in these studies. But at what price? The extinction of our closest relative? How much should a chimpanzee suffer to save a human? You must appreciate that suffering isn't pain. It's the emotional response to perceived pain. Fear causes suffering. Anxiety, the fear of what the future may bring, is a more complex cause of suffering. Primates, in my opinion, suffer greatly when they perceive that their pain is without end. A chimp can live for fifty years. You've been locked up, so I imagine you can relate to what I'm saying better than most. Anyway, until we as humans accept that primates have a similar response to suffering as humans, we'll subject them to the cruelest forms of torture. Whether in the name of science, social good, or God, it makes no difference. I don't condone murder, but I don't condone genocide either, and that's what the human animal has visited upon the primates."

Jerome gave me his card, his hand trembling with anger. "Call me in a few days, and we'll talk again."

"I'm not sure what I should do," I said.

"Nor am I," replied Jerome as he turned and walked away.

CHAPTER
F O U R

My trip to the zoo had produced more questions than answers. Having considered the possibility that Kikora was stolen, I had rationalized away the consequences. But I hadn't imagined that a scientist had been murdered in the process.

I called Gus Jaynes. Gus was the FBI agent whose testimony had sealed my criminal conviction. Two and half years after my trial, a few of the witnesses who had testified against me recanted. When Gus learned he'd been lied to, he fought to have my conviction overturned. He was ultimately successful, but was kicked out of the Bureau as a reward for being principled. The Bureau made up reasons for his termination, but the bottom line was that Gus had caused the justice machinery to forfeit a conviction.

From my perspective, the criminal justice system frequently has more invested in winning that it does in rendering justice, finding truth, or engaging in any other noble enterprise. After thirty years of dedicated service, Gus simply didn't belong. He's now a private investigator and a good friend. I told him about Sydney's visit, her disappearance, and Kikora, and did my best to allay his concerns that I'd lost my mind. I asked if he could check his sources for any information about Sydney and the death of Dr. Celia Stone and get back to me. We agreed to meet for dinner in Georgetown at a bar called the Bent Note.

I stayed at the zoo until early evening watching the orangutans and gorillas. Around seven, I joined the weekend bar traffic heading down Wisconsin Avenue. I turned off Wisconsin at R Street and made my way toward Georgetown University. By chance, I found a parking space on N Street and parked my old Honda between a BMW and a Mercedes. I took my trumpet case from the trunk and headed down the street.

Georgetown offers an eclectic mix of cultures. The wealthy live in restored townhouses and newly constructed condos. Some are public figures, their pictures routinely appearing in *The Washington Post*. They frequent the pricey restaurants and drive expensive cars. Georgetown is also a bar and disco oasis, attracting the newly affluent looking for a mate, the suburban teenager looking for adventure, and the social dropout looking for a stage on which to flaunt his or her indifference. Most of the street traffic is confined to M Street and Wisconsin Avenue. But even blocks from those streets, there's a smattering of purple-haired girls and blue-suited males.

Georgetown also offers cuisine to satisfy any palate. Despite the ever-present exhaust from diesel buses, the fragrances wafting from the kitchens of a dozen small restaurants are hard to miss. Chinese, French, Italian, and Spanish cuisines join in a perfume that titillates the appetite. The Bent Note features a Cajun style of cooking—blackened fish, shrimp Creoles, and soups that could revive the dead. I picked up the restaurant's peppery scent a block from where I parked and two blocks from the stairs that led to the dark and refreshingly damp cellar where the Bent Note was located. By the time I reached the bottom of the stairs, I was hungry, and I was hot for the blues.

I spotted Greg Binh, a second-generation Vietnamese-American, warming up on bass. I had originally hooked up with Greg through his brother, Tony, whom I met in prison. Tony, an excellent guitarist, had patiently taught me chord progressions, riffs, and bends.

Unfortunately, Tony wasn't as good at check forging, and was serving a five-year sentence. I was beside him when he died of a stab wound to the stomach. The minimum-security facility where I was incarcerated was relatively safe but not immune to power struggles and politics. Violent, convicted felons sometimes cut deals to serve their time at what the defense bar calls a "club-fed." Although I never learned what prompted the attack, I do know that the inmate who committed the stabbing left the facility in a horizontal position, just like Tony.

Greg nodded as I approached. "Shep man," he said. "The blues-playing lawyer man. Gots to be torn to play his horn."

His singsong mannerism wasn't an act. I had grown accustomed to it, but when we first met, I had found it grating.

Wally Mercer and Teaki Stroud appeared from behind the stage. Wally played keyboard and Teaki played drums.

"Play me a tune, law man," said Greg. "Play me a tune about summer time."

I opened my trumpet case. Ripping through a few scales, I found a good key and began a slow rendition of "Summer Time." Greg added a running bass and Wally and Teaki joined in. I'm not a great musician by any stretch of the imagination, but even I can get lost in the music I make. Emotions that I can't express verbally are bared in my horn's brassy voice and echoed by the instruments playing around me.

When the last note was played thirty minutes later, I looked around and the place was packed. Applause erupted from the crowded room, but as polite as the gesture was, it was unnecessary. We weren't playing for the benefit of the assembled customers, but for ourselves. The approval I needed was in the "oh yeahs" that came from Greg, Wally, and Teaki. If the audience enjoyed it, that was okay too.

I spotted Gus at a table in the back, sitting next to a man with large glasses and a gray ponytail. Gus and I shook hands, but his cohort kept his eyes on a gin and tonic. "You sounded pretty good," said Gus.

I nodded a thank-you, and waited for the man with the pony-tail to acknowledge me. Finally, he leaned forward. "Music like that is too sad," he said. "Life is sad enough."

"Shep," said Gus, "meet Mel."

Mel glanced at me but took no notice of my outstretched hand. He had an unhealthy look to him. Large dark bags hung from below his eyes, his nose was bulbous and fleshy, and his skin was scarred by acne that still blistered his cheeks and forehead. His face looked stretched, like a football with eyes.

"Anyone hungry?" I asked, motioning to a waiter.

"Food here's too hot," said Mel. "I don't eat hot food in the summer."

I ordered a blackened grouper and a salad. Gus did the same. Mel quizzed the waiter on what other entrées were available. When the waiter departed, Gus said, "Mel knows a lot about groups—gangs, organizations, causes, that kind of thing."

Sources, or snitches (depending on your perspective), are a breed unto themselves. What they know and how they know it is a mystery.

"I'm looking for Sydney Vail," I said.

"You and a helluva lot of other people," responded Mel, who then belched.

"And why might that be?"

He shrugged. "'Cause." I wasn't in the mood to play this game, so I just stared at him. Finally he said, "Vail took a chimp from a sci-entist lady, supposedly to find the chimp a home. The cops want Sydney because the scientist lady ended up dead. The group Sydney works with wants the chimp. The company she stole the chimp from wants the chimp back. And with the chimp tied to a murder, Sydney Vail's got no place to go with the chimp, so one way or the other she's in deep shit."

I heard myself groan. "How did the cops connect Sydney to Stone?"

Mel seemed irritated by the question, as if the effort to speak required more energy than he cared to expend. Someone should have told him that snitches are paid to talk. After a few moments of practiced indifference, he said, "The day Stone's body was discovered, the local police charged a guy named Jonathan Freeman for the murder. Freeman was already in custody for busting up a lab at Doring Research. A few days later, Freeman was released and arrest warrants were issued for Vail. Freeman and Vail are members of the Wildlife Defense Council. The WDC operates on a cell level, meaning the members of the local organization don't know the members of the other cells. That way, if they get busted, the damage is limited. Contact is made through a Web site that sends out coded messages to cell leaders. Apparently, taking the chimp was Vail's gig and Freeman wasn't happy about it. Rumor has it that he fingered Vail. He wanted the credit and the media exposure."

"Any idea if Vail actually killed Dr. Stone?" I asked.

"I can't say for sure," answered Mel. "Lots of stories, but nothing reliable."

"Vail's rap sheet is lengthy, but mostly minor stuff," said Gus. "She was arrested for assaulting a woman at a traffic light. Apparently, the woman threw a cigarette butt out the window and Sydney handed it back to her. The charges were later dropped."

"Which proves nothing," offered Mel. "Vail is a nut case. She's on the run. That makes her look guilty even if she isn't."

I leaned back in my chair. It was now obvious to me that Sydney wouldn't be coming back for Kikora. What wasn't clear was what I should do with the chimp.

The food arrived. I savored the grouper, but Mel spent most of the meal picking at his hamburger and whining that it tasted like fish. Fortunately, he left before I throttled him but not before Gus committed him to finding out more about Sydney and Jonathan Freeman. Gus and I had dessert and coffee while the band played its first set. At the break, Gus suggested we go outside and take a walk. I paid the bill, grabbed my trumpet, and headed toward the exit.

The outside air was damp and fresh, cleansed by a passing storm. Car tires hissed against the wet cobblestones that paved the street outside the bar. I sensed Gus had something he wanted to say, and a few minutes after we left the Bent Note, he proved me right.

"You don't like being a lawyer, do you?" he asked, shaking his head. "At least, you don't any more."

"Why would you say that?" I replied. "I've got clients. Building a practice takes time, especially if you've been disbarred."

"I didn't say you weren't trying to practice law. I said you didn't like it." He made a sucking sound through his teeth. "What you like is investigating. You're good at it."

"I got three people killed investigating Reilly's murder," I said sharply. "I don't think that qualifies me as good."

Gus peered in the dark window of an art shop. "Consequences are handled by your conscience. Your instincts compel you to ask questions. Your distrust of the system makes you question the answers. You're like a moth drawn to a flame. Resisting is going to make you miserable. If you like, I could teach you the trade. You could work for me."

To my surprise and consternation, I found the prospect of working for Gus enticing.

We reached his car. "Think about it," said Gus, opening the driver's door. "In the meantime, you better figure out what to do with that chimp of yours. If Sydney's connected to the murder of Celia Stone, a prosecutor might decide that you are too."

I spent the weekend considering my options, but without resolving anything. I also worked on client matters and waited to hear from Sydney, at least by phone. I began to think I was waiting for Godot.

On Monday, Robbie Owens, my office mate, returned from her vacation. Robbie and I are the same age, and both of us are divorced. Robbie was a childhood friend that I played with on my many visits to see Reilly. She's retained her tomboyish charm and is still eager to join me on hikes and fishing trips. We had resolved the boundaries of our relationship on my return to Lyle last Christmas, meaning we were friends but nothing more. I spent the morning listening to stories and the afternoon catching up on cases. Then I told Robbie about Kikora.

"How do you get involved in these things?" she asked.

I shrugged. "Good karma?"

Because caring for Kikora occupied more of my time, Sydney began occupying more of my thoughts. By Wednesday, it had been ten days since Sydney arrived with Kikora. I kept my concerns to myself until Frieda brought up the issue while making lunch. "If Sydney doesn't call by tomorrow, she's in trouble. So what are you going to do about it?"

Problems are like stray cats. Sometimes they come to visit and go away, and sometimes they stay and adopt you. "I don't know," I said. "For one thing, I'm not sure it's my problem. And even if I let you bully me into thinking it is, I'm afraid that asking around could draw attention to Kikora." I immediately recognized the inherent contradiction in these two statements. Having admitted I was worried about both Sydney and Kikora, I couldn't legitimately deny that Sydney's whereabouts weren't my problem.

Frieda chopped a stalk of celery. "Not if you were a reporter," she offered without looking up.

"But I'm not," I said.

"But you know someone who is," countered Frieda.

Frieda was referring to Cali McBride, a reporter who had lived with me for a few months on the farm, until last spring.

"Yes, I do," I said. "But I can handle this myself."

Frieda walked away mumbling something about men and donkeys, but I didn't stay for a clarification. I walked outside, where I found Cecil and Kikora playing tug of war. Suddenly, Kikora ran toward me, making a flying leap into my arms. "Why don't you get some lunch?" I said to Cecil. "Kikora and I will go for a walk."

I put Kikora down and tried signing the word "play" the way Carrie had taught me. Kikora returned a puzzled look until I realized I'd used the wrong hand position. I signed to her again. She responded with a hoot, then took my hand.

My farmhouse—the old poor farm—occupies the southeast corner of a property that's almost a perfect square, one mile on each side. Kikora and I walked behind the barn and up a dirt track overgrown by weeds.

A decade ago, tractors made their way along this road to fields that produced corn, potatoes, and melons. Today, the tractors are rusted hulks, and the fields are home to birds and bugs and stands of wild locust and sassafras trees. Lynn Run, which meanders along the northern two-thirds of the poor farm's eastern property line, is home to frogs, turtles, and several varieties of trout. I shuddered to think how close this little piece of paradise came to being sold, bulldozed, and paved over to allow a mall to be built.

Kikora found the field exciting and intimidating. She ran ahead on all fours until she disappeared in the tall grass. Moments later, she stood erect so I could see her, then she dove back into the grass and disappeared. On one foray into the grass, I dropped to my knees and snuck up on her. The game was on and we played until we reached a rocky area, where the tall grass couldn't grow.

Kikora found an anthill and busied herself harassing its residents. She was eating them one at a time, a slow and inefficient process. I tried to show her how to use a stick to get more ants to eat, but she wasn't interested, probably because I wasn't eating the ants I collected. While we were busy prodding and poking the anthill, I heard my cell phone ring. It was Gus. "Mel confirmed that Sydney Vail was arrested last night and is on her way to the Leaks County court for a preliminary hearing," he said. "She's been charged with the murder of Dr. Celia Stone. Stone was working with chimpanzees for Doring Medical."

"Damn!" I said.

Gus groaned. "The report doesn't mention a missing chimp, but the implication is there. You've got to get rid of that chimp, Shep. You hear me? You can't fool around with this any longer."

Kikora and I headed back to the farm. She played the hide-in-the-grass-game and chased butterflies while I watched, wondering what the future held for her—and me.

CHAPTER
F I V E

W hen Kikora and I returned, Carrie was on the porch waiting for me or, more precisely, for Kikora. She held an apple in her hand and Kikora ran to her. "Not until we put on a diaper," said Carrie while simultaneously signing. The two of them strolled off hand-in-hand. I sat in the porch rocker and forced myself to think about the implications of Sydney's arrest.

Immediately after Sydney left Kikora with me, I minimized the legal risk that I would be charged with possessing stolen property. But murder was a different matter. Police and prosecutors love conspiracies, and that made an accessory to a felony charge more likely. The authorities were already looking for Kikora. Whether they could trace Sydney to Reilly and ultimately to me was unclear. As much as prosecutors are prone to see conspiracies, ex-cons like me are inclined toward paranoia. I actually looked up to see if a cruiser was coming down the dirt driveway.

My self-interest wasn't my only concern. Even though I'd only met her briefly, I was having trouble believing that Sydney would kill anyone, even to liberate an animal she thought was being abused. I was still mulling over Sydney's arrest when Carrie returned.

"I can see trouble on your face, dear," she said, sitting down next to me. "Trouble always likes company. How about you tell me what you're wrassling with?"

I repeated what Gus had told me, and Carrie listened quietly. "So what will happen to Kikora?" she asked.

I chose my words carefully. "If the police determine that Kikora is here, she will be returned to the labs at DMI."

Carrie nodded, then seemed to focus on something off in the distance. "When I was three or four, my parents gave me away." A smile crept on her face, a translucent smile that couldn't quite mask the pain in her eyes. "At least I think they were my parents."

I was stunned for a moment. "You always said you were born here," I said, more than a bit puzzled.

She shook her head. I could see she was fighting back tears. "I made up that story because I couldn't bear to think that my mother didn't love me, didn't want me. I still can't."

I took her hand and squeezed it. "You don't have to…"

"Thank you dear, but it's time I told someone the truth." She looked at me. "The people who gave me away were the first people I remember living with. I assume they were my parents, but the Lord only knows for sure. They gave me to some people who I believe were relatives. I stayed with them for a year, and then *they* gave me away. I couldn't talk because I was deaf. All I could do was grunt some, which is why everyone thought I was stupid even though I understood everything that was said to me. Finally, I was deposited at the entrance to the farm and told to walk to the end of the driveway. I had a little tote bag and the clothes on my back."

I was unsure what had provoked her to tell me about her past. Carrie promptly cleared up the confusion.

"At the farm, I was excited to be with other children, people who were also unwanted for one reason or another. Finally, I was with my own kind in a place where I belonged. I read in the information Sydney left that Kikora had been raised by a couple in their home and was sold because she was becoming too strong, too difficult to manage, and too much trouble. So at the age of two and a half, she was sent to a lab, where she was locked in a small cage. It must have been terrifying to go from a caring family to a place where they poke you with needles and make you sick. Now she's here with us. I don't want

her to go back to that research place. In the book that Sydney left—
All One Family—they mentioned that there were sanctuaries for chim-
panzees. Maybe Kikora could go to one of them—some place where
I could visit her. Can you help make that possible?"

"I don't know, Carrie. But I'll try."

She nodded, then stood. "I thought you would," she said, giving me a kiss on the forehead. "I'll bring you the book so you can get
started." She thought for a moment. "Now that I've told you the truth
about me, I'd be appreciative if you wouldn't go telling anyone else."
I nodded, and she hurried away.

I spent the rest of the afternoon in my office in Lyle searching
the Web for information about the murder of Dr. Stone. The murder
took place on July 24. Sydney arrived at the farm on August 1 and had
now been missing for ten days. The murder marked the violent end of
several days of demonstrations outside the grounds of Doring Medical
protesting the use of chimps as test subjects. According to local news
accounts, Jonathan Freeman, a "known eco-terrorist" and animal
rights "militant," had led the demonstrations. Freeman was promptly
arrested for trashing a lab at DMI and then charged with the murder
of Dr. Stone. On August third, two days after Sydney visited me at the
farm, all charges against him were dropped, and he was released. The
Commonwealth's Attorney for Leaks County declined to explain why.

DMI is a publicly-traded company led by Howard Doring, its
founder and board chairman. Doring apparently believes that human
beings have every right to exploit all other living things. He defends
testing on chimpanzees as a scientific necessity. In Howard's words,
testing is a "right of the evolutionary victor." He once proposed that
with genetic manipulation, primates could be raised like cattle to provide humans with blood and replacement organs. Howard also rationalized testing on prisoners and the retarded (he referred to them as
"defectives"). A decade ago, he published a paper suggesting that within the human species were subspecies, some less evolved and less
deserving than others. Howard denied that this was a racist statement

and has since defended his conclusion.

Before her murder, Dr. Celia Stone had been the top scientist at Howard Doring's DMI. She had used primates in various studies, one of which had resulted in a drug for treating Alzheimer's. The drug was pulled from the market two years after its release because of side effects that had not shown up in the animal tests or in the human trials. Apparently, the chimps metabolized the drug differently than humans, and the human trials were too short in duration to reveal the drug's dark side. Despite the problems with the Alzheimer's drug, Dr. Stone continued to use chimps for biomedical research and was intending to use them in tests of a new anti-obesity drug developed by DMI.

The news of Dr. Stone's death caused DMI's stock to drop by thirty percent. Apparently, investors were concerned that with Celia gone, the testing of the company's new anti-obesity drug would be delayed. The stock recovered most of this loss following the company's media blitz, committing to the start of anti-obesity drug tests by the end of August. The drug was to be tested on chimpanzees first, then on humans.

From other Web sites, I learned that one of the largest sponsors of testing on chimps is the U.S. National Institutes of Health. NIH had contracted with DMI on a number of occasions to test AIDS vaccines. NIH continued to use the facility after the U.S. Department of Agriculture cited DMI for violations of the Animal Welfare Act. One article even accused NIH of buffaloing animal rights groups into supporting a federal law, entitled the "Chimpanzee Health Improvement, Maintenance, and Protection Act," and referred to as the "Chimp Act," that was intended to provide sanctuaries for chimps who are retired from testing. According to the article, NIH initially opposed the legislation, hoping to persuade animal rights groups to commit their support for it. (If NIH didn't like the proposed law, the others would see it as good for chimps.) After the animal rights community invested substantial resources in lobbying for the Chimp Act, but before it passed, NIH used its political weight to amend the legislation. As enacted, the Chimp Act grants NIH lifetime access to any chimp entering the sanctuary system. While the law refers to granting chimps "sanctuary," the system created by the Chimp Act has more to do with warehousing chimps for NIH than it does with creating a retirement home for abused chimpanzees.

The fate of many of the retired chimps was almost too sad to read. Either because of a lack of facilities or a lack of concern, many of these human-sized test subjects spent years in isolation in small cages. Many went mad, biting themselves and chewing off fingers. I recalled what Jerome had said about primates and suffering. Part of me wondered if the chimps who died were better off than those who survived.

Reading about what might happen to Kikora if she were returned to DMI left me restless and on edge. I noticed that Frieda was ignoring me because, in her words, I had become "ornery and useless." I finally told her about Sydney's arrest and my suspicions about Kikora's origins. She became irate, leaving me with a clear directive, "So what do you intend to do to make sure Kikora doesn't go back?"

I had been ruminating on that question for days and still had no answer. I said something that made little sense to Frieda or me, and she walked away mumbling something I'm sure I was better off not hearing.

That night, I finally began reading *All One Family.* I had intended to skim it, but once I started reading it, I was hooked. I fell asleep after reading half the book. The next morning, after a night of bad dreams that stirred up old memories, I informed Frieda that I would be at my office in Lyle so I could catch up on work. I didn't have anything pressing, but I needed to escape the farm for a while, and I wanted to finish *All One Family.* Before I left, I noticed that Carrie was acting suspiciously coy, which generally meant something was going on.

Robbie was out visiting a client, so I expected to have the

office suite to myself. When I arrived, I found the soft glow of my computer monitor reflecting off the back of my chair. The chair began to turn slowly until the light fell on the sweet face of Cali McBride.

"How was that for dramatic effect?" she asked. "I saw it in a movie."

"In the movie, the person in the chair was dead," I said, leaning against the doorjamb. "What are you doing here?"

"I'm here to help," she said.

"I don't need any help," I said.

Cali shrugged. "Then I was just passing through."

"No one just passes through Lyle, at least not anyone with a real destination in mind."

She smiled, her soft green eyes holding my gaze and reminding me of the first time I laid eyes on her. Cali was tall and athletic and very much cat-like in the way she moved and held herself. What made her appealing to me was that she was kind and smart, tenacious and caring. Like most felines, she also could be a brat whenever the mood struck her.

"I heard you had a problem," she said, adding, "Carrie sends me an email from time to time." Cali propped her feet on my desk. "I'm looking for a story. You have a chimp you acquired from someone who has been arrested for murder. Murder can make good copy. You should have shared this with me, you know."

"Carrie shouldn't be telling anyone about a chimp, most certainly not in an email, and without question not a reporter. How's Brad?" I asked.

"Bradley is fine," she said, emphasizing the last syllable of his name.

"How can you like anyone who insists on calling himself Brad-*ley*?"

She twisted a lock of hair around her finger. "I like him because he doesn't carry a gun and doesn't get himself shot at. He's very considerate, a bit quiet but interesting, and he likes a lot of things I do. I think he's the most patient man I've ever met."

"I think I hear a 'but' in your voice," I said.

Cali sighed. "He wants me to meet his family."

"Oh, my," I said.

"It's a complication for sure. You seeing anyone?"

I gave her a "none-of-your-business" look and said, "I'm not lonely, if that's what you're asking."

We stared at each other for a moment, accepting the other's explanation. Finally, Cali said, "Tell me about the chimp and the dead scientist."

I didn't answer.

"You know I'll annoy you until you tell me."

"You'll annoy me even if I do," I responded. She crossed her arms and set her jaw.

"All right," I said. "Take your feet off my desk and your tush out of my chair."

I took control of my desk. "First, you'll have to sign a non-disclosure agreement, meaning you can't go publishing what you learn without my permission."

Cali looked at me incredulously. "You're kidding! You want me to sign something that says I won't blab about what we find?"

A few keystrokes and the printer whined. "I might want to argue that Sydney is my client so neither you nor I can be called as witnesses. I don't want to waive the attorney-client privilege."

"I don't believe this," she sputtered. "I know you were trained to be an asshole, but that's no reason to act like one."

I put the document in front of her. "It's not your fault, but you're trained to be a reporter and a snoop. Sign here," I said, pointing to the signature block. Cali signed the document, and I slipped it into a folder.

"I'll give you the highlights, but no questions and no story based on what I tell you."

Cali stayed quiet while I described Kikora's arrival and Sydney

Vail's legal situation. Then she said, "So we have an animal rights activist who steals a chimp, a scientist who liked to perform experiments on them and is now dead, and an eco-terrorist who was originally charged with killing the scientist, then set free. You've got the chimp and want to find out what the story is with Sydney Vail, but you can't go nosing around because someone will connect you to the chimp and take her away, maybe arresting you in the process."

"That's the gist of it," I said wearily.

Cali gave me a big-time smirk. "But I can nose around because I'm a reporter."

"I don't recall asking for your assistance and don't actually want it," I said.

She pulled her chair up to my desk. "I suspect that's true, so we should cut a deal."

"I don't cut deals with reporters."

Cali screwed her face into a pout. "That wasn't nice." A moment later, she smiled. "Come on. It'll be like old times."

I rubbed my eyes. "Our old times lasted about four months, three of which I spent recovering from a gunshot wound."

Cali nodded. "Good point. But you know it'll be easier having someone do the legwork. Besides, I need a really juicy story. We'll both win." I hesitated. "You know I'm right," she said.

I heard the soft padding of feet and the sad cry of a large gray cat that had taken up residence in the office. Jumping on my desk, he gave Cali a wary look, then settled on top of the folder and purred loudly. I rubbed him under his chin, taking care to avoid the twisted and gnarled flesh that was once his left ear. "This is Van Gogh," I said. "According to the vet, someone removed part of his ear with a knife. Van Gogh likes to tell everyone about it."

She pointed her finger at Van Gogh's nose and waited for him to rub it with his forehead. "I can't believe anyone would be that cruel," said Cali.

"If people weren't cruel to animals, we wouldn't need laws

making animal cruelty a crime," I responded.

Having made his presence known, Van Gogh jumped off the desk, found a spot on the floor illuminated by a sunbeam, and began bathing himself in the warmth.

"So, did Sydney Vail kill Dr. Stone?" asked Cali.

"I don't know," I said. "I don't want to believe she did, but she might've killed her in a rage or something."

"You know who she is, don't you?" Cali asked. I shook my head. "Sydney was a gorgeous soap opera star. A few years ago, she got involved with an anti-fur group that threw red paint on twenty thousand-dollar fur coats. One night, Sydney answered a knock on the door of her apartment. She lived in a secure building, so she thought it was a neighbor. When she opened the door, someone tossed acid in her face. She lost her looks and her acting job. I hadn't heard anything about her since." Cali again tormented a lock of hair, a sure sign she was thinking. "Now, Sydney Vail reappears after years of hiding, kills a scientist, and steals a chimp," she mused. "That would be quite a story, wouldn't it?"

It would, only I hoped it wasn't true.

CHAPTER
S   I   X

Cali spent most of the day at the farm with Carrie and Kikora. I stayed in my office and finished *All One Family*, then went over the material I'd pulled from the Web. The more I read about the treatment of chimps, the more sympathetic to Sydney's objective I became. I couldn't quite justify murder, but I wasn't morally outraged by her theft of Kikora either. I might feel differently if I were arrested as an accessory, but for now I was definitely in the Kikora-Sydney corner.

I spoke with Gus, who told me that Sydney had denied knowing Celia Stone, then changed her story when confronted with DNA evidence. "Harvey Raimer's been appointed by the court to defend her. He defended Jonathan Freeman, the man originally accused of the murder."

I looked up Harvey's number and called him to set up a meeting. He wasn't keen on the idea, but was even less interested in arguing about it on the phone. Finally, I secured an appointment for Monday morning and hung up the phone.

Sunday afternoon, Cali showed up with a picnic basket and we took Kikora to the stream for lunch. "What's new on our case?" she asked.

"It's not *our* case," I said. "I have an appointment with Harvey Raimer, Sydney's defense counsel, tomorrow in Byron's Corner."

"What a coincidence," said Cali. "I was going to go to Byron's

Corner myself tomorrow to see what I can learn about Celia Stone. So, you can drive, and I'll just be myself."

"Sounds like I should plan on being medicated," I said.

We spent the afternoon playing with Kikora, inventing new games for her and bribing her with fruit and sweets. At times I found myself watching Cali more than Kikora. For an instant, I remembered standing opposite her in the snow on Christmas Eve, her incredible green eyes drawing me closer until our lips touched for the first time, a blissful moment that hours later would be followed by bloodshed and death.

All of this violence was precipitated by my insistence on knowing who had killed Reilly Heartwood. These events have haunted me for months, and occasionally still slip into my dreams.

As I contemplated where that first kiss might have led, a thunderstorm ended our picnic. We just made it back to the house when the rain broke. As we scurried onto the porch, Cali fell against me. She lingered for a moment, gave me a puzzled look, then pulled away and ran to her car. I toyed with running after her, but the impulse never gained strength. As she drove away, I realized that what might have been might never be. I dealt with this new reality like I did most other unpleasant things—I just decided not to think about it.

After dinner, Kikora and I looked through magazines. She enjoyed seeing pictures of animals and dresses. She signed at the pictures, although I had no idea what she was saying. She was also quite vocal. A dress she liked was a single hoot. A really nice dress got two hoots. Kitty cats were popular, too, but dogs were not. We were having a good time when we came upon an advertisement featuring a woman dressed in a white coat. Kikora studied this ad for a long time, then went over to her bed and got out her blanket. To my astonishment, she crawled under a table and began rocking back and forth. I could do nothing to coax her out. Then, I remembered what Jerome had said about suffering. For thirty minutes I talked to Kikora, assuring her that everything was going to be all right. When I left, I wondered if I'd also been trying to reassure myself.

That night, I barely slept. I first dreamt about Cali. Then, in the middle of the night, I awoke, bent on imagining how Sydney might have murdered Dr. Stone, then how Sydney might have acquired Kikora without being involved with Stone at all. It's hard to sleep when your brain is playing the possibility game with no facts to constrain it. Somewhere in the early morning, I must have given up, because when the alarm went off at six, I was wrapped in a deep sleep that I didn't want to end. Gradually, I pulled myself from bed, made a pot of coffee, showered, dressed in my best suit, and headed to Heartwood House.

Heartwood House is situated on a hill high above town on a fifteen-acre tract of land. The house was originally constructed after "The War of Northern Aggression." (Sarah Mosby, Reilly's sister, taught me not to refer to the war of rebellion as the "Civil War.") The house's original owners were the Abernathy's, a powerful and wealthy family that controlled Lyle and most of Morgan County. The Abernathy dynasty ended when the modern generation dissipated the family fortune. Rose Abernathy, the last of her clan to reside at the Abernathy family home, even spent some time at the poor farm. Reilly bought the Abernathy family home at a tax sale and spent a considerable sum restoring and modernizing it. The purchase was just one of many controversies that surrounded Reilly until his death last December.

Frieda, the residents, Lora Jean Brady, and a dozen cats make Heartwood House their home. The house also serves as a temporary shelter for needy individuals while more permanent housing is located. On this day, there were no transient visitors and Lora Jean was away at summer camp.

Cali was standing in the driveway when I pulled up. She was wearing round designer sunglasses, a dark pantsuit, and a soft cotton v-neck blouse. A warm breeze lifted locks of her auburn hair. She set them in place with a toss of her head, only to have the wind play with them again. With the stately Heartwood House as a backdrop, Cali radiated a casual elegance that bespoke money and class. Replace my old 1992 Honda with a new Beemer and the two of us could be members of the horsey-set about to attend a nearby wine tasting or an equestrian show.

"How do I look?" she asked, slipping into the car.

"Like a moneyed woman," I said, "with a dash of *décolletage* and a hint of sensuality."

She parted her lips slightly. "Only a hint?" she said with a coquettish flair.

I pushed a thought from my mind, and started the engine. "Buckle your seat belt," I said. "This car has only one airbag and it's on my side."

"That doesn't seem fair," she responded. "If you hit something, what am I supposed to do?"

"Puff out your cheeks?" I asked facetiously.

Cali wasn't amused. "When we get back, we're going to shop for a new car with all the safety features. You know you can afford it, so I don't want to hear any excuses."

A comment about shopping flashed through my head, but I decided against sharing it with Cali. She seemed satisfied that she'd gotten the last word, and we left Lyle and headed to Interstate 81.

Two weeks had passed since Sydney's first visit to the farm, and I began the trip with a mixture of dread and curiosity. Cali asked how arrest warrants were issued but quickly tired of my scholarly answer and began fiddling with the position of her car seat. I took the hint and ended the lecture. A few minutes later, Cali asked a more meaningful question.

"What do you think about biomedical testing on chimpanzees?"

The question was the one that had occupied my head most of the night. "It isn't what I think about testing on chimps that is important, but the fact that you can pose the question that way at all."

"Sometimes you even sound like a lawyer," said Cali. "What did you just say?"

"In the eyes of the law and most religions, animals are property, and to a large degree the owner of the animal can do what he or she wants to it. Despite what we are taught as children, all life isn't sacred or we wouldn't eat meat, wear leather shoes, or cut down trees. The value of life is actually relative, not absolute. We don't care what we do with rats because they are considered vermin.

"The problem with chimps is that they are our closest genetic relatives. They live long lives, are social like humans, have a culture all their own, and have the ability to communicate with us through sign language. Yet historically, scientists treat them like rats. We test on them, then lock them up in small cages for the rest of their lives. When we project humans into that situation, we get morally outraged and make noises about 'human rights.' We don't talk about testing on humans any more because humans, whether retarded, evil, or socially undesirable, have rights. Because we don't recognize that chimps have rights, we are free to ponder the question of whether it's all right to test on them, and we are free to pose the question in a way that gets the answer we desire. The bottom line is that chimpanzees aren't entitled to be treated like humans because humans decide who is—well, human."

"Wouldn't you be in favor of testing on chimps if it would have saved your mother?" pressed Cali. "Or what if we could figure out why chimps don't get AIDS? Wouldn't that make the sacrifice of chimpanzees worth the price?"

"You should have been a politician," I replied. "That's supposed to be the magic question, but the question is inherently unfair. If the life of someone who was important to me were at stake, I might be willing to justify testing on anyone or anything—including prisoners, neighbors I don't like, and the retarded. But of course those options aren't available because we've defined them away. If we conclude that chimps are entitled to the same basic rights as humans, we basically eliminate the option of testing on them, too."

"It's all so confusing," said Cali. She thought for a moment, then asked, "What will happen to Kikora if she goes back to DMI?"

"Kikora will either die as a result of the experiments performed by DMI or go mad in a cage," I replied. "If the tests of DMI's new anti-obesity pill are successful, lots of overweight people will be better off."

Cali threw up her hands. "What's this about an anti-obesity pill?"

"I'm sorry," I replied. "I thought I told you. DMI has developed what appears to be a revolutionary pill that controls the way the body metabolizes fats and sugars. They are testing it on chimps to determine at what dose heart and liver damage occurs. The chimps that don't die from the tests may be euthanized and autopsied."

"Kikora is going to die so I can eat cheeseburgers without gaining weight?" asked Cali, her voice dripping with outrage.

"That's one perspective," I replied, "but not really the point."

"You're going to lecture me about something," said Cali disparagingly. "I can feel it."

I shrugged. "You can be lectured or you can be ignorant."

Cali folded her arms across her chest. "I'm listening," she said tensely.

I cleared my throat. "I read on the Internet that one in every three adults in the U.S. is now obese, and nearly two-thirds of all American adults are overweight. We are getting fatter by the minute, despite spending billions of dollars on dietetic junk food. Even our kids are getting fat. What this portends is a significant increase in diabetes, high blood pressure, heart disease, and kidney failure. Life expectancy for obese people is substantially lower than for the rest of the population. Children today may not live as long as their parents. And recently, obesity has been linked to cancer. I think the number is something like one in seven cancer cases caused by being overweight—something like 90,000 preventable deaths each year. The latest study even linked obesity of pregnant women to birth defects."

Cali was quiet for a moment. "Okay. So an effective diet drug isn't frivolous. But it still seems to me that we are killing chimps because we eat too much and don't get enough exercise."

"Maybe," I responded, "but with all the talk about exercise and diet, we are still getting fatter. A pill may be the only answer." I glanced at her. "I didn't say it was fair. I'm just saying that the health benefits of an effective weight loss medication are enormous—at least if you're a *Homo sapiens.*"

Cali threw up her hands. "Now I'm really confused. Are you saying that we shouldn't test on chimps at all, that we should only test important drugs on them, or that we should test anything and everything on them as long as we treat them better after we're done with the tests?" she asked.

I glanced at her. "I definitely wouldn't kill a chimp for a better roach killer, but I don't know if all testing on primates should be banned or not. I just don't."

"Well, let me know when you figure it out," she responded.

We settled into another silence, broken finally by Cali's attempt to find a radio station that played her kind of music. She eventually gave up and fell into a light sleep. I turned on the cruise control and followed the wide ribbon of asphalt through the picturesque Virginia countryside, rehearing Cali's questions and my answers. Chimps were property, I'd said. As I looked out over the rolling farms of the Shenandoah Valley, I could hear one of my Virginia ancestors saying the same thing about slaves.

We were just south of Staunton when Cali woke up and asked, "How come you didn't call me?"

I glanced at her. She was staring out the window. "Carrie told me you were happy and busy. I figured if you needed anything, you'd let me know."

"That's not much of a reason," she said.

I shifted in my seat. I wasn't comfortable with this discussion, but accepted it as unavoidable. "You left because you said you had to get away to forget what happened Christmas Eve and because I wasn't coping. By the time I'd worked through everything, you were in Chicago with Bradley. You were content. I was putting the pieces of my life back together. I just thought it best to leave it that way. You didn't call me, either," I added.

"No, I didn't," she said.

That was the last word until we arrived in Byron's Corner.

Byron's Corner is a small town of 1800 residents in the middle of the Shenandoah Valley. The main road is Maple Avenue, and numerous other streets are named after varieties of trees and flowers. I had visited the town a dozen years or so ago to attend a blue grass festival held on a farm nearby. I recalled the town as old and tired, with buildings in disrepair and streets littered with trash. As I cruised down Maple, I was struck by how much the place had changed. With the arrival of DMI five years ago came a new prosperity. The shops were quaint, the street was clean, and the cars and trucks that lined the street were new and shiny.

After a few minutes driving in circles, I stopped and asked directions, a decision that evoked admiration from Cali. While I drove, Cali read a local newspaper story about the Stone murder. The article vilified Jonathan Freeman as a "known anarchist and eco-terrorist" and characterized Sydney Vail as a "radical animal rights extremist," suggesting, if not saying outright, that her reputation qualified her as the killer. Stone, by contrast, was a preeminent scientist who had "dedicated her life to finding cures for the worst diseases to afflict humankind." She would be "sorely missed by her friends at DMI, where she worked, and even by those who didn't know her."

Cali tossed the paper into the backseat. "I really like objective reporting, don't you?"

"Gee," I said. "I thought you wrote that."

"Very funny," replied Cali.

We found the law offices of Harvey Raimer on the top floor of an appliance store. The entrance was at the back. Stepping inside, I was first struck by the smell of things old and musty. My first visual impression was that the office had been vandalized. Papers were strewn everywhere. File cabinet drawers were open, their contents spilling out onto the floor.

A heavy-set man appeared from the back. He looked ancient. Drooping eyelids and dark puffy bags encircled his eyes, and fine red lines meandered across the pale yellow skin of his cheeks and nose. Sparse white hair hung above his otherwise bald head like a plume of smoke.

"Harvey Raimer?"

When he smiled at me, his countenance changed, and his face brightened. We introduced ourselves. "I've heard of you," he said looking at me. "You're that attorney who solved the murder of Reilly

Heartwood." To Cali he said, "And you wrote about it."

"That's right," answered Cali.

"I liked the way Reilly sang a song," mused Harvey. "You know, I met him once at a concert down the valley a piece." Harvey seemed lost in thought. "I haven't done anything to attract the attention of a reporter in a long time. Can't say the experience was favorable, but I can't hold that against you, now can I?" He turned and walked away.

We caught up with him in a small closet. He fed a stack of papers into a shredder and turned it on. A minute passed. He looked at us again. "So you want to talk to me about Sydney Vail? She's my client, you know, and I'm sure you appreciate that I can't discuss the case with you, especially in front of the media."

"Cali is here in her capacity as research consultant," I replied. "Nothing you tell us will be printed until you waive your attorney-client privilege or it becomes public information."

He studied us for a moment. "I didn't want the Vail case," he said. "I was actually thinking about retiring. I settled the Freeman case for a good sum of money. At least to me it was a good sum. The next day, I suddenly saw this pig-wallow for what he was, and my life for what it wasn't. When I agreed to defend Sydney, I decided the least I could do was to try and clean up the place."

"You cut a deal to spring Jonathan Freeman?" I asked.

"I did," replied Harvey. "It's a good story, but you'll have to feed me if you want to hear more."

Harvey led us to a restaurant less than a five-minute walk away. Though it was only a few blocks from his office, Harvey was breathing heavily by the time we arrived. Even allowing for the heat, I wondered if Harvey would live long enough to enjoy his money.

After we ordered, Harvey pulled a pint bottle of whiskey from his pocket and placed it flat down on the table. He stared at it for a moment, then gave it a spin. When it stopped spinning, the cap pointed at the door.

He spoke without looking up. "I used to play this game every day. Every time the bottle would point at me, begging me to open it, I opened it. Then I got the Freeman case. I played the game, but somehow I knew if I took a drink, Jonathan Freeman would either rot in jail or be electrocuted. Maybe that's why the Commonwealth's Attorney gave me the case."

I started to ask a question, but Harvey waved me off. "I started my practice in a county south of here," he said, his eyes focused on the bottle of whiskey. "I had a good thing going—even had aspirations of running for Commonwealth's Attorney. Then I defended a rape case. I won, but my client was guilty. He raped another young girl a week after the trial. My practice dried up. I blamed myself, even though the justice system is designed to let a certain number of guilty defendants go free. I lost my confidence, then I lost my house, my friends, and my family. I came here and found that drinking was a good way to avoid thinking and feeling. I got used to taking crumbs from other attorneys and working traffic court. Hugh Strong—he's the current prick who's pretending to represent the people of the Commonwealth—throws a few cases my way, subject to an unspoken understanding of how I will handle the defense. I get paid, and he gets to add a victory to his résumé. Most of my clients are guilty, so the arrangement doesn't usually distort justice. But a capital offense, like the one that Freeman was charged with—that's a big deal."

Harvey went silent, lost in some train of thought that didn't involve us. I broke the silence with a question. "You were assigned to Jonathan's defense?"

Harvey looked at me and nodded. "Hugh Strong offered a deal of second degree murder and malicious destruction of property. No burglary or the like. Freeman would serve twenty years with no chance of parole. The first thing I said to Freeman was that the plea bargain seemed fair. I didn't say hello, or offer him my hand, or introduce myself. I didn't ask him any questions. I just laid out the deal. I was scared, you see, of having the responsibility for another man's life. That's a lot of pressure for a drinking man."

Harvey bit his lower lip. "Freeman didn't say a word. He just stared at me with this strange look on his face—like a frightened animal. Then he did his best to tell me he didn't kill Celia Stone, but I wasn't listening. You should have heard his voice. He barely croaked out the words. And then the absurdity of it all struck me. He'd been charged with a capital offense, and I was chawing at him like he'd gotten a ticket for speeding. So I asked him if he killed Celia Stone. He said no. He told me his side of things, and I left the cell determined to defend him."

"I'm not following you," said Cali. "You said something about a deal."

"Truly an amazing thing," he said reverently. "I decided to do what I was hired to do, to defend my client. I did it well, too. I started to ask questions. I reviewed the security tape from the lab that Freeman was supposed to have broken into. DMI made it public as part of their campaign to discredit the protesters. The more I watched it, the more it looked like he'd been set up. Then I learned that Freeman had been under surveillance by the feds. His alibi for the murder was an FBI report that had been given to the prosecutor's office. I started to ask DMI about the FBI report and the video, and a few days later we were talking a deal—on my terms. Not just a deal to get Freeman off, either. I started making noises about false arrest, defamation, and anything else I could think of. They let Freeman walk and they wrote a check—a big check—and I got a third of it. The only condition was that we not talk about what happened at the lab and that we assist with the investigation."

"Let me guess," I said. "They wanted to know who stole a

chimp."

Harvey eyed us suspiciously. "It's not public information that a chimp was stolen."

I ignored his comment, and said, "Freeman told you about Sydney Vail, and you passed that information to DMI and the police. So what made you decide to defend Sydney?"

"I'll answer that question when you tell me why *you're* here," he replied.

Our food arrived and I described the now familiar story of Sydney and Kikora's arrival at the farm. "The police are looking for a chimp," he said. "Sydney paid for gasoline on a credit card at a station just outside Lyle. My advice to you is to give up the chimp before you get into serious trouble."

"What kind of trouble?" asked Cali.

"Shep could be charged as an accessory to felony theft and even charged with murder," answered Harvey. An image of prison once again flashed through my mind, and it made me cringe. "This is serious stuff," said Harvey. "They'll figure it out eventually. I think you can avoid prosecution if you come forward on your own."

Cali gave me a worried look. "I don't like the sound of this at all."

I knew Harvey was right, but I wasn't ready to think about it.

"We've gotten off the subject," I said. "You haven't told us why you decided to defend Sydney."

Harvey ran his hand over his mouth. "This sounds trite, but I took the case because I felt I owed her. I told her that my former client was instrumental in her arrest. I'm not sure if, by taking her case, I've violated the code of ethics, but frankly I don't care. She's okay with it."

"Do you think she killed Stone?" asked Cali.

Harvey smiled at her. "A reporter's question, Ms. McBride,

and one that I don't care to answer. I will tell you that the evidence against her is damning. The police have blood evidence from the scene. DNA from blood found at the murder scene matched the DNA in a sample of Sydney's hair taken during a search of her house. They'll get a warrant for a blood sample soon enough. In a few weeks, the grand jury will issue a true bill—an indictment—for murder one. There'll be an arraignment where I'll have to enter a plea. So far, the prosecutor doesn't want to talk about a deal. I'd say Sydney Vail's in deep trouble."

"I'm sure she has a story," I said. "I'd like to hear it—from her."

"Me, too," agreed Cali.

Harvey shook his head, then looked at Cali. "I can't let a reporter talk to her," he said. "I could present you as co-counsel," he said, turning to look at me, "but that'd be a stretch. First, you're a material witness if not a co-defendant. Second, if the cops don't know you have the chimp, you'll be helping them figure it out. I will take you to see Sydney, but you better be prepared to surrender the chimp tomorrow or the day after, because I'm certain search and arrest warrants will be issued by then. It's your call."

I looked at Cali. "I want to help you," she said to me, "but I don't know what to say."

"Well then, that makes two of us," I said.

Cali pressed her hands together as if in prayer. Worry and fear were etched in her face. "I don't want you to go to prison," she said. "After all you went through, I couldn't bear it."

I racked my brain for an answer that I knew wasn't there. I was certain Kikora would die a hideous death at DMI, but there was no law prohibiting such treatment. Kikora *belonged* to DMI. She didn't own herself because in the eyes of the law, she had no self. Everything I'd read and learned about primates contradicted this simplistic conclusion, but the law wasn't required to be rational. Any attempt to protect Kikora would fail and most likely send me back to prison. And that was, of course, the bottom line. Prison frightened me more than anything in the world—even death. Whatever else might be at stake, the choice was binary: send Kikora back to the lab or go to jail.

"I'd like to talk to Sydney," I said.

I handed Cali the keys to my car. "Check out DMI and see what you can learn about Celia Stone. I'll go with Harvey to the jail. We can meet back here in a few hours."

"You sure you want to do this?" asked Harvey.

I wasn't, but I said I was.

CHAPTER
SEVEN

The Leaks County jail is twenty minutes from Byron's Corner. Harvey signed me in as co-counsel for Sydney Vail. After fifteen minutes, we were escorted inside. The concrete and steel facility seemed to get smaller and more confining the deeper we penetrated it. When we emerged from the maze and arrived at an interrogation cell, an alarm sounded, reverberating off the concrete walls. The damp air, slightly scented by the smell of urine, disinfectant, and stale cigarette smoke, was suddenly all too familiar, stirring old memories and resurrecting old fears. The deputy beside me pulled on the steel bars and the door slid noisily to the right. Harvey stepped inside, but I, still lost in past remembrances, hesitated for just a moment.

"You got a problem?" asked the guard.

I noticed Harvey staring at me. "And they say you can't go home again," I quipped while joining him.

My entrance to the cell was marked by a thunderous crash of metal against metal. The guard nodded. "You holler when you're ready to leave," he said.

A moment later, Sydney Vail, clad in prison orange, her hands shackled to a belt around her waist, shuffled into the room. Before her capture, Sydney had been confident, almost arrogant. She had survived her disfiguring injuries and the loss of her acting career. She was used to making demands *and* getting her way. The woman who entered the cell was none of these things. Her stare was empty.

Confusion and doubt were written all over her face. Less than a week in a cell had taken the fire out of her. I'm certain that she'd spent her nights here sleepless, contemplating a lifetime behind bars. If convicted and sentenced to time, Sydney would have to adapt to survive. At that moment, she was in transition from free woman to state prisoner, and the transition was consuming all her strength.

"Hey," she said, her voice fearful but welcoming. "Are you helping with my defense?"

"Something like that," I answered.

A guard removed her shackles and led her to a table. "Take your time," he said to Harvey and me, "but no physical contact."

Harvey and I sat opposite her.

"Is everybody okay?" she asked.

"Everybody is doing fine," I said, responding with a forced smile to the indirect reference to Kikora.

Harvey gave me a disapproving stare, then said to Sydney, "You need to tell Shep what happened on the day Dr. Stone was murdered."

She rubbed her temples. "We have contacts at a lot of the labs. I got a tip that Celia Stone was caring for a lab chimp at her home, so I phoned her. Celia was pretty messed up. She wanted to save Kikora, but she didn't want to lose her career. It took me a while to get her to trust me, to convince her that I wasn't a crackpot and was really trying to help Kikora. We talked on the phone a lot, but Celia didn't want to meet me. I didn't pressure her, but I didn't let her off easy either. She blew hot and cold. But then the experiments were scheduled to begin. DMI had a press conference and all the protocols were set. Celia panicked. She demanded that I come and get Kikora before it was too late."

"Celia Stone called you from her home or from her office?" I asked.

"I think it was from a pay phone," answered Sydney.

Harvey groaned softly, then looked at me. "I asked the phone company about getting records of pay phone calls, but they haven't been very helpful."

"What about Jonathan Freeman?" I asked. "How was he involved?"

Anger flashed in Sydney's eyes. "Jonathan is a publicity freak. He wanted to get the chimp himself and hold a press conference. A local cell manager overruled him. Do you know how cells work?"

I nodded and she continued. "Anyway, Jonathan wasn't happy about running a diversion, but he went ahead with the demonstration, and even broke into DMI." She rubbed a mark on her wrist apparently made by her restraints. "I went to Celia's the morning of the demonstration to pick up Kikora. The police and everyone were out at DMI watching Jonathan parade up and down screaming about things he doesn't understand. Celia was upset, which upset Kikora. When Celia tried to hand Kikora to me, Kikora became frightened, and the three of us struggled. All the while, Celia was crying and Kikora was whimpering. Celia ended up scratching me, and so did Kikora. Celia told me to come back later, that she would sedate the chimp. When I came back, Celia was dead. I found Kikora hiding behind a couch rocking back and forth very slowly. She didn't resist when I took her. She didn't seem to care."

"What time did you go back?" asked Harvey.

"I picked up Kikora around five."

The story was plausible, but unconvincing. "Did you wear gloves or wipe away your fingerprints?"

Sydney shook her head. "I wasn't stealing Kikora. A vice president of DMI was giving her to me. Why would I?" Sydney stared into my eyes. "You believe I'm innocent, don't you?"

According to basic legal principles, the defendant is innocent until proven guilty. A complementary principle is that the government carries the burden of proving that the accused is guilty. Even so, I had little doubt that these principles did not apply to Sydney Vail. Because of who she was, she was convictable of almost any charge. All a prosecutor had to do was bombard a jury with Sydney's public statements about the righteousness of her cause and the moral imperative of using any means necessary to accomplish her objectives. The jury would see Sydney as a fanatic who deserved to be behind bars. If she got lucky, Sydney would be sentenced to life without parole.

So, despite the prevailing legal principles, Harvey and I would have to convince a jury not only that Sydney didn't commit or couldn't commit the crimes with which she was charged, but that each member of the jury would rot in hell unless he or she voted to acquit. The odds of accomplishing this task were small, and largely dependent on what evidence we could produce.

"To be fair, it doesn't matter what we think," answered Harvey. "What we have to decide is whether the jury will believe you. If we believe they will, no problem. If we believe they won't, then we need to talk about our options."

We sat in silence for a moment. "You once assaulted a woman at a traffic light," I said. "Tell me about that."

Sydney laughed. "I didn't assault anyone," she said. "This woman tossed an ashtray full of cigarette butts out her car window and onto the street. I merely retrieved them for her and threw them back into the rear seat of her car. Somehow, she thought old butts weren't litter. I mean, how arrogant can you be? Anyway, she saw my face and freaked. The cops thought I hit her, but I didn't."

I nodded. "I won't plead guilty to something I didn't do," she said.

"I know," I said. I did know, because I'd once said precisely the same thing to *my* lawyer. I could have taken a plea bargain, admitted I was guilty of defrauding the government, and served a six-month term. I didn't, and was instead sentenced to twelve years. Sydney was playing a game with much higher stakes—life in prison, or death. I wasn't sure she could afford to take the morally right position.

We sat silently for a moment. Then Sydney shook her head. "You will take care of things?" she said more as a demand than a question.

"It's complicated," I said.

I felt Sydney's eyes boring holes into me. "I trusted you," she said through clenched teeth.

Her response angered me. "You disappeared without a word," I said, "exposed me and my friends to a significant legal risk, and you want to talk about trust?"

"Everybody calm down and shut up!" demanded Harvey, but it was too late for that.

Sydney stood up. "Don't do this! You son-of-a-bitch. You have to protect her!"

"You're asking me to go back to prison," I said. "I can't do that."

A moment later, Sydney threw herself across the table and tried clawing at my face, her nails barely missing my eyes. "You bastard! You lousy bastard!"

A guard appeared and tried to pull her from me, but Sydney resisted. Finally, another guard arrived, and doused her with pepper spray. The two guards dragged her from the cell screaming. Moments later, the Leaks County jail resonated with clangs and rumbles and, buried in the background—or perhaps in my imagination—were the mournful mutterings of its inmates.

CHAPTER
E I G H T

A few minutes after the guards removed Sydney Vail from the interrogation cell, Harvey and I exited the Leaks County Jail.

"That went well," I said. "Don't you think?"

Harvey didn't take the bait and ignored me. I called Cali on my cell phone. For lunch, Harvey suggested a restaurant called the Country Kitchen. Harvey, I was learning, liked to eat.

As Harvey and I stepped inside the restaurant, we were treated to a rush of cool air laced with the fragrance of fresh bread, spices, and coffee. Cali waved from a table in the back and we joined her. "Let's keep our voices down and not say anything we might regret having overheard," said Harvey.

Cali looked at me. "You don't look happy. Did you tell Sydney about your decision?" I nodded. "I gather she didn't take it well." I nodded again.

"Let's order," suggested Harvey. "Then we can compare notes."

Cali and Harvey discussed each item on the menu, with Cali listening attentively to his critique. I found this distracting and frustrating, until I heard his review of the smoked baby-back ribs cooked dry, with a vinegar sauce on the side.

Our orders placed, I outlined Sydney's version of how she happened to be at Celia Stone's house on the day of the murder. "At first it sounds convenient," Cali said, "but it also sounds too complicated to make up."

"Not to a jury," said Harvey shaking his head. "No one around here is going to buy it for a second."

"Unless we can prove it's true," I countered.

Cali wagged a finger at me. "Funny you should say that."

She was interrupted by the arrival of our waitress with plates of food. "Who ordered all of this?" I asked.

"We did," said Cali impishly.

All meaningful conversation stopped. We ate, then pushed our plates aside as dessert arrived. While a waitress poured coffee, Cali tapped a spoon on the table, a troubled expression on her face. I thought she was going to comment on the food when she said, "According to the newspapers, Dr. Stone was well liked and," Cali made quote marks with her fingers, "will be sorely missed by everyone. Yet, DMI and the local prosecutor knew Freeman didn't kill Dr. Stone, but they tried to make it look like he did. It seems to me that DMI management cared more about finding someone to blame for the murder than finding the right culprit."

"Maybe DMI realized that finding the murderer was going to be impossible," I said. "Murders committed by strangers are hard to solve. If the stockholders were anxious, a way to calm them down would be to solve the crime quickly, without an investigation and a lot of publicity. Jonathan was a good patsy. He was a believable suspect, and no one around here was going to ask any questions. Of course, no one counted on Harvey's having a fit of conscience and exposing the fiction for what it was. With Jonathan Freeman locked up in a corrections facility in Richmond, the threat of more protests here would probably have faded away. If he took the plea, no one would ever see the evidence that cleared him. In that sense, the identity of the real killer was irrelevant."

Cali scowled, her forehead creased by deep furrows. "Is everything about money?"

"Money and winning," I said. "Diet pills are a huge business. If DMI has discovered an all-you-can-eat antidote, they could be looking at a regular cash stream of countless billions for years."

Cali picked at a piece of piecrust. "Maybe we should try a few of those pills and order some more dessert."

I managed to snatch a pecan from her plate while avoiding a hand slap.

"Get your own," she snapped. "Anyway, what I was trying to explain was that, in actuality, Celia Stone was not universally adored."

"You got into DMI?" asked Harvey.

Cali shook her head. "No. Two minutes after parking my car, I was captured and dragged off to security. A man named Arthur Collins interrogated me for a few minutes, gave me a warning, and escorted me back to my car. I asked him how Jonathan Freeman could walk into a lab and destroy it without being detained, but Collins ignored me. Frankly, I found him a bit creepy."

"You lost me," I said. "You went to DMI and got thrown out. Not exactly a victory for the good guys."

"True," she said, "but I managed to learn where the employees hang out for lunch."

"You ate lunch before you came here?" asked Harvey.

"For the sake of fitting in while gathering some information, I just had a little salad," said Cali, "but you're missing the point." She pulled out her PDA and touched the screen with a stylus. "The point is, Celia ran a real tight lab. She fired people routinely. One lab employee, a Henry Thomas, when fired in March, made quite a scene and had to be removed by security. So much for her being missed by absolutely everyone."

"A woman who pisses off employees is sure to have other ene-mies," I said.

"Once I got the conversation started, it was hard to keep track of all the stories," continued Cali. "By my count, Celia was involved in four civil suits against her neighbors. The police were called a number of times to remove her from local establishments for one reason or another. She seemed to like to abuse waitresses so much that she couldn't get a meal in most of the local restaurants other than carry-out. And she may have had a thing going a few years back with a lowlife named Devon. I didn't follow all the conversations too well. I was concerned that I might be asking too many questions, so I didn't press it, but it's a start. The bottom line is that Celia could piss off a piece of wood. She really was a bitch."

"I couldn't call a woman a bitch," I said.

"And your point is?" responded Cali.

"You are good," said Harvey with sincere admiration.

"Thanks," said Cali, "but I'm not done. Apparently, Stone wasn't getting along with Arthur Collins, the head of security at DMI. Someone said something about the two of them having words a week or so before Stone was murdered. Don't know what it was about, but all wasn't happy at the lab."

I found myself buoyed by the prospect that there were other people with possible motives for killing Stone. Harvey tempered my optimism with legal reality.

"The information is interesting and may even be meaningful," he said. "But DNA evidence is going to be hard to overcome. Even if God testified Sydney was in heaven at the time of the murder, her DNA puts her at the murder scene. That Sydney's skin was found under Stone's fingernails just about closes the door on any kind of defense short of finding the killer and making him or her confess. You also need to keep in mind that Virginia is a jury sentencing state and has the death penalty. Women aren't usually executed, but Sydney could be regarded as a terrorist. Unless we can mount a decent defense, if only to mitigate the charge of first-degree murder, she's looking at life without parole. But none of this is important at the moment. What we should be talking about is Shep's problem."

Harvey was referring to Kikora. "Maybe I can buy Kikora," I said. "Maybe DMI will sell her to me, and I can find her a nice sanctuary with other chimps."

"That's an idea," said Cali.

Harvey shook his head. "DMI can't afford to sell a chimp that's part of a test protocol. The stockholders have been promised boats full of revenue from recurring drug sales resulting from those tests. Selling one of the protocol chimps may send the market a signal that DMI is abandoning its business model because they've lost their lead scientist."

"But it would be great public relations," I countered. "The chimp that Dr. Stone died to rescue from terrorists is rewarded with its freedom."

"That's not bad," agreed Cali. "I have friends in the press…"

"Stop!" snapped Harvey. "You're missing the point. You make an offer to return the chimp that is in any way conditional and you're going to be served with a search warrant and an arrest warrant. It's too dangerous a game. Return the animal, then offer to purchase it if you want to." Harvey stood up. "I have to go, but please take my advice. There's no point taking a moral position that you can't defend."

I watched him leave, aware that Cali was staring at me. "What are you going to do?"

Stone was dead. Sydney, if she were lucky, was facing life behind bars. And the helpless animal they both wanted to protect would most likely die in an experiment so that humans could live longer no matter how much they ate. "I have no effing idea," I said, "but I'm still taking suggestions."

Cali and I drove away from Byron's Corner in a torrential downpour. Lightning bolts hit the ground nearby as if aimed at us. Small hailstones drummed against the roof of the car and smacked the windshield. I thought I'd taken a detour through hell when suddenly the car was flooded with sunlight and the sky ahead turned blue and cloudless. But the gloom inside the car remained. Cali coiled and uncoiled a lock of hair while resting her head against the window. She was quiet for a while. "It's strange," she said. "I'm a good reporter with a compelling story about a chimpanzee, a woman accused of murder, and an attorney forced to choose between his own self-interest and the life of a chimpanzee."

She turned to me. "And for the life of me, I just want it to have a happy ending."

CHAPTER NINE

The sun was toying with the tops of the mountains as we pulled onto the dirt road leading to the farm. Cali and I had fallen into a long silence. I had said what there was to say and wasn't eager to rehash any of it. She seemed to have accepted the fact that talking about the issues wasn't going to change anything.

When we arrived at the house, Frieda greeted us as we stepped onto the porch. "So? Did you find out anything about Sydney?"

I tried to force a smile, but I doubt my expression masked my apprehension. Cali turned away and went inside. "Yes and no," I said. "I'll explain later."

Frieda, who isn't known for being touchy-feely, grabbed me by the shoulders. "I haven't seen you like this since just before your mother died," she said, her voice thick with worry. "What happened?"

"Give me a few minutes," I said.

"It's bad news, isn't it?" pressed Frieda.

"It's bad, and I can't talk about it right now," I said, and went to my room. I changed into cutoffs and a T-shirt, then went out the backdoor to find Kikora.

I passed Harry Drake, who was fastening an old tire to a rope draped over a tree branch. "Kikora's going to like this," he said proudly.

"She will," I said approvingly, knowing full well she'd probably not use the swing for long.

Carrie appeared from behind the bunkhouse with Kikora in tow. Kikora, carrying a bunch of wildflowers, nibbled on the blossoms. When she saw me, she threw the flowers down and broke into a run. In a flash, she launched herself into my arms, almost knocking me down. She studied my face, touching my cheek with her finger. Then she put her hands on her cheeks and pulled them down. She did this several times.

"What is she saying?" I asked Carrie, recognizing that Kikora was signing, but not recognizing its meaning.

"She's asking if you're sad," said Carrie. "Are you?"

I stroked her head, then signed "no."

Carrie looked at me, and immediately understood that I was lying. Kikora signed something I didn't understand, then wrapped her arms around me. A moment later, she jumped from my arms, grabbed me by the hand, and led me to the field behind the equipment barn. She signed "chase," then ran into the tall grass and hid. It took me a moment to realize she was trying to cheer me up by playing the hide-in-the-grass game.

I managed to play with this marvelous creature for a few minutes until I just couldn't overcome the dread of events to come. As she frolicked and hooted for my benefit, I was struck by the enormity of what would play out during the next twenty-four hours. Intellectually, I knew that Kikora had to be returned, that the law gave me no choice. The laws of property were established during several hundreds of years. The Virginia courts would respect the rights of Kikora's owners and return her to DMI. Any attempt to deny DMI its rights would not only be futile, but criminal conduct punishable by *the law*.

As I watched Kikora dart in and out of the clumps of grass, I couldn't help admire her resilience. Kikora's cumulative experience with humans had been one betrayal after another. With what we know about primates, and chimpanzees in particular, about their ability to feel and think and perceive much like humans, and about their ability to feel pain and to suffer as we do, I couldn't quite fathom how we could be so indifferent to the emotional suffering we cause them. Basically, we excuse the pain because we discount the suffering. Until recently, doctors routinely operated on newborn humans without anesthesia because we thought they couldn't suffer. In her thoughts and behavior, Kikora was not unlike a human child. If we treated a human child the way we planned to treat Kikora, the child protection advocates would be screaming "child abuse."

When Kikora and I returned, Harry, Frieda, and Cali were sitting on the porch, their heads bowed, their eyes averted. Carrie stood by the door, a tissue in her hand. I could hear sniffling and knew that Cali had explained what had transpired in Byron's Corner and what it meant.

"Why do we do such cruel things to helpless creatures?" sputtered Carrie.

"Because we can," said Harry.

I handed Kikora to Cali. Frieda looked at me. "There's no other way?" she asked.

I ignored the question, then went inside and called the Leaks County police station. "I need to talk to the detective in charge of the Stone murder investigation," I said.

After a minute on hold, a voice came on the line. "Detective Mason speaking. How may I help you?"

I didn't respond. I hesitated at the brink, then closed my eyes, willing myself not to speak, to hang up the phone. I heard the detective's voice again, then the hiss of the phone line. "I believe I have the chimp that was stolen from DMI," I said finally. With those words, I sealed Kikora's fate and mine.

"You must be Shep Harrington," he said. "I was working on a

search warrant for your place, and an arrest warrant naming you as an accessory to murder. I'm awfully glad you called."

"Yeah," I said.

"You did the right thing, Mr. Harrington," said the detective.

"For me, anyway," I said.

I hung up the phone and met the others on the porch. "I think you should all go back to town," I said. "The police and DMI will be here in the morning. I don't want you implicated in any legal action that might come from having Kikora here."

Cali began to protest, but Frieda cut her off. "Shep is right. There's no benefit in staying here. We need to get on with our lives."

"Are you going to be all right?" asked Cali, her eyes glistening with tears.

I nodded. "I'll manage," I responded.

"Kikora likes to be brushed before she goes to bed," said Carrie, sobbing. "And she likes to look at magazines."

"I know. I'll take care of her."

Harry tried to speak but couldn't. In all the years I'd known Harry, I'd never seen him cry. I was relieved when all of them finally climbed into Frieda's van and drove back to town.

Kikora and I played games until it was time for her to go to bed. I brushed her, then brought her my latest magazines. There was no way I was going to sleep. I made coffee and watched Kikora via the Web cameras I had bought and Harvey Drake had installed. The picture was quite good. I found a remote that allowed me to select a camera, see around the room by moving it, and then focus that camera within a narrow range. I heard a beeping sound, and noticed that two VCR's next to my computer were recording Kikora's antics. Kikora flipped through the pages of two magazines before stopping to look at a picture in the latest issue of *Time*. She briefly signed at the picture. I found the camera with the best view and moved it with the remote until I determined that the picture was an advertisement depicting a woman in a white lab coat. The ad was for health insurance. I pulled back to capture Kikora's image. I had no idea what she was saying to the picture, but I was fascinated nonetheless.

I went to get a refill of coffee. When I returned, Kikora was hitting the magazine with a toy baseball bat. I couldn't hear her, as there was no microphone hooked up to the camera, but it was clear she was upset by something. I went to her room and found her under her bed. I decided to leave her there, then retrieved the magazine from the floor.

Creased by repeated blows from the toy bat was a picture of a gray-headed man in a dark suit, a cane in his lap. The caption above the photo read, "HOWARD DORING: TROUBLE AT DMI?"

I got down and looked at Kikora, who peered back at me from under her blanket. "I wish I could talk to you," I said. "I don't know how you know what's going on, but somehow..." I didn't finish the sentence. I was just too tired.

I climbed into Kikora's bed and closed my eyes.

I awoke before sunrise. Kikora, already awake, was playing with her dolls. To my surprise and relief, she let me change her diaper without chasing her around the room. I left her for a few minutes, then returned with her breakfast. Kikora watched me, aware that something in her routine had changed but unsure what. She ate her cereal and fruit, and studied the piece of chocolate I offered her for dessert. She loved candy—considered it one of her favorite treats—but this was the first time anyone gave it to her for breakfast. She was right to be suspicious. The candy was laced with tranquilizers Sydney had left behind. Finally, I reached for the chocolate, but she snatched it off the highchair and popped it into her mouth. I checked to be sure she'd eaten it, then waited for the drug to take effect.

Fifteen minutes later, she stopped playing with her dolls. I could see she was fighting the sedative, though unsuccessfully. Then she acted on her suspicion that something bad was going to happen. She grabbed her blanket and crawled under her bed. When I looked at her, I saw the fear in her eyes. She curled up in a fetal position and rocked back and forth. I rolled away from the bed and lay on my back staring at the ceiling. For a moment, I felt as if somebody was removing my heart from my chest. I thought about feeling guilty, but the feeling didn't stick. For all the compassion and empathy I felt for Kikora, her situation was not my fault. What was gripping me wasn't guilt but anger—at Sydney, at the law, at the DMI's of the world.

I had experienced this kind of anger only once before—when accused of committing fraud against the government and tried as a liar and a cheat. Financial considerations—of my company—had dictated that I go to prison. My employer traded my freedom so it could continue to do business with the Defense Department despite having violated the government's procurement laws. Kikora's freedom was to be traded so that DMI and its stockholders could earn millions—maybe billions—of dollars on an anti-obesity drug. She had no advocate to question this exchange. Under the law, she had no rights at all. She was a powerless, rightless non-entity, alive but still property. The more I thought about her situation, the more indignant I became.

Somewhere in these mental gyrations, an odd thing happened. I found myself formulating a legal argument why Kikora needn't be returned to DMI. Soon, puzzlement turned into relief. I had changed my mind.

CHAPTER
T E N

Energized by my decision to resist Kikora's return to DMI, I called Harvey. After eight rings, I became convinced he wasn't home. But two rings later, I heard his sleepy drawl. It took him a moment to realize who I was. "Do you know what time it is?" he asked.

"Not really," I replied.

"I guess that makes it better," he said. "It's five in the morning and you want what?"

"I'm going to file a motion this morning in Morgan County Court to have my arrest warrant and search warrant quashed. I'm also going to ask to be granted custody of Kikora as her guardian so DMI can't seize her."

Harvey was suddenly awake. "Don't do this, Shep. DMI won't cut you any slack if you fight them. They'll have you thrown in jail."

"If Kikora weren't a chimp, but an abused, retarded child, would you feel the same?"

I heard Harvey exhale slowly. "You have a lot of guts," he said.

"No, Harvey, I don't," I replied. "Lots of people have been fighting to protect primates for years. I'm just in this one specific situation, trying to make it come out right. I'm afraid to go to prison, but afraid to live with myself if I don't do something to help this chimpanzee. When I say it out loud, it sounds crazy even to me."

"I hope you know what you're doing," he said, then changed the subject. "What do you know about the circuit judge for Morgan

County?"

"Judge McKenna was a friend of Reilly's and my mother," I replied. "I don't see him often, except when he comes to fish Lynn Run. I think he'll grant me a hearing."

The line went silent for a moment. "What's your argument that Kikora is entitled to the court's protection as a person, not as a thing?"

"I don't know yet," I said.

"Should make for an interesting hearing," replied Harvey. "Let me get some coffee. I'll take care of things on this end. How do I get to your place?"

I gave him instructions. Before he hung up, he asked, "Are you sure you want to do this? Have you really thought through all the consequences?"

"I'm done thinking about it. I want to get on with it. How's Sydney?"

"She's still upset about Kikora. She spent the night in the infirmary at my request," said Harvey. "The warden's a friend of mine. They'll keep an eye on her so she doesn't do anything stupid."

I hung up the phone, then called my officemate, Robbie Owens, at home. Despite the early hour, she answered on the first ring. "Jet lag," she explained. "You in trouble?"

I went through the short version of what I wanted to do. "Jesus," she said, "I wasn't gone long enough for you to get into this big a mess. Let me do some research, and I'll call you back." She gave me the number of Judge McKenna, and I hung up.

I began searching the Web. I found more animal rights Websites than I could assimilate. I read a half dozen appeals for animal rights grounded in ethical and moral arguments. What I needed was a sound legal argument anchored in legal principles and case law. I'm certain a needle lay somewhere in the cyber haystack, but I wasn't fortunate enough to find it.

I left my computer and dialed the number of Judge James Markham McKenna. As his phone rang, I wished I knew him better. He answered the phone with a simple "Yes?"

"Judge McKenna, this is Shep Harrington. I'm sorry to bother you at this hour..."

"If you think you woke me up, you're wrong," he said. "But if you're thinking a call this early bothers me, then you're dead right. What do you want?"

"I want you to issue an order quashing a search warrant and an arrest warrant," I replied.

"You've shot someone, have you?"

"Not yet."

I heard him laugh. "Lots of people out there deserve shooting," he said. "But as a judge, I can't be deciding who they are. So what kind of trouble are you in?"

I told him the whole story. To my surprise, he listened patiently. "Listen to me, son," he said finally, "as a friend of your mother. You're in a peck of trouble. I don't see any legal basis for you not surrendering the chimpanzee, and I can see a lot of arguments for throwing you in jail if you don't. Unless you tell me you have an argument that goes against two hundred years of precedent, I'd be rethinking your position."

"I'm sorry, your Honor," I said, "but I've been rethinking my position for most of the last twenty-four hours. As to an argument, I'm working on one right now."

I heard Judge McKenna mutter something under his breath. "I know the magistrate in Leaks County," he said. "I'll discuss the warrants with her. And I'll give you a custody hearing, but you must agree to voluntarily surrender the chimp should I rule against you. Because the matter involves a wild animal, I'm going to hold the hearing on the poor farm, where the animal is located. You will also grant me permission to fish Lynn Run after the hearing. I'm sure the water's too warm for the trout to be hitting, but I'm feeling lucky." I tried to thank him, but the line went silent. I hung up the phone, then called Heartwood House. Cecil answered, and I patiently explained what I was up to. I could hear Carrie and Frieda demanding to know what was going on.

"Shep's going to quash the warrants against him," he shouted, "and he's going to ask the court to name him Kikora's guardian. Exactly what does that mean?"

Suddenly I heard Cali's voice. "What are you doing?"

"I'm doing what I should have done all along," I replied. "I'm a lawyer. I'm going to act like one. Kikora is now my client."

After explaining the pleadings to Cali, I asked that she bring Carrie to the farm to watch Kikora. I made coffee and then outlined a legal argument based on the constitutional law I remembered from school. Robbie called and we edited what I had written, adding a few new ideas, removing what sounded weak and, as Robbie put it, "cutting out what sounds like liberal whining."

At 9:30, I spotted the dust cloud rising from an approaching car.

The first to arrive was Judge McKenna. He was wearing blue jeans and a shirt bearing the picture of a trout. He looked the way a seventy-year-old man should. His face was sunken and his skin was speckled with age spots. His hair was white and thin. As he ambled up to the porch, I noticed a slight hitch to his gait. He offered me his hand and gripped my hand firmly. "Reilly was a good friend," he said. "From what I've heard, you've done him proud. Lots of young people would have taken his money and wasted it. Now let me meet your client."

I took the judge to the bunkhouse. Kikora was still groggy from the medication I'd given her, but I coaxed her out from under the table and picked her up. "Judge McKenna, meet Kikora."

Kikora wrapped her arms around Judge McKenna's neck and pulled herself to him. The judge didn't resist, even as Kikora latched on to his glasses. "She's everything you said she was," he said. "But is she a person under the law who is entitled to a legal guardian? The question challenges the wisdom of our most revered philosophers and the tenets of many religions."

Carrie appeared at the door, followed by Cali, Frieda, and the others. Carrie took Kikora outside. Frieda volunteered to make coffee while the twins, Larry and Cecil, agreed to help the judge arrange chairs on the porch.

Cali took me aside and hugged me. "You look tired," she said. "And I'm so proud of you, but I can't bear the thought of you going back to prison."

"Then I need to win," I said with more confidence than I felt.

I spotted Robbie and listened as she chatted with the judge about fly-fishing. Harvey, who had arrived unnoticed, talked to Carrie and gawked at Kikora. At 10:45, another cloud of road dust announced the arrival of more visitors. Emerging from the dust was a three-vehicle armada—a black Lincoln, a stretch limo, and a police cruiser.

The cars emptied quickly. The lawyers were easy to spot in their white shirts, dark suits, and shiny black shoes. The limo driver stepped from the car and opened the passenger door. A moment later, a man dressed in a light-colored suit emerged, holding a cane adorned with a large lion's head. When he reached the porch, the man stopped, faced me, and said, "I'm Howard Doring. I believe you have something that belongs to me."

Doring, according to the media, was in his seventies, but the man before me seemed younger, and he was fit and vigorous. Unlike many men his age, including Judge McKenna, he stood straight, with no curve to his back or slope to his shoulders. A thick, well-groomed mane of snow-white hair lay atop a deeply tanned face, suggesting he may have spent more time on a golf course than in an office. He held himself as if expecting to be observed while maintaining an air of indifference. I disliked him immediately.

A burly black man stepped from the police cruiser, his eyes covered by dark aviator glasses, and a Smokey The Bear hat on his head. "Detective Reggie Mason," he said offering me his hand after joining me on the porch. "I'm pleased to meet you. I gotta tell you, the story about you finding Reilly Heartwood's killer was pretty awesome. I also read about you getting sent to jail 'cause people lied at your trial. I kinda feel like I know you some." I found his affable nature odd considering that he might have to arrest me after the hearing.

Howard studied me, his jaw muscles flexing. "I am not a patient man," he said coldly. "I don't like people interfering with my business or my things. I've lost my most valuable scientist. I have a lab that I need to refurbish. I have a very important protocol that I need to start. Give me back the chimp you stole and let me get back to work."

I ignored his demand. "Have you ever taken a moment to get to know the chimps you experiment on?"

Doring looked at me as if the question was beneath him. "Why in God's name would I want to do that?" he asked. "I don't get to know the rats or the mice I kill either. Do you get to know the chickens you eat for dinner? Do you want to save them as well?" Laughter erupted from the gaggle of dark-suited lawyers who had accompanied Howard Doring. "Let's get on with your little morality play so I can get back to work."

"In due time," said Judge McKenna. "But first we have to have a hearing."

One of the suits stepped forward. "My name is Jeff Miles," he said. "I'm general counsel for DMI. I have to say that I find this hearing objectionable and irregular."

"You don't have to say anything, counselor, until I ask you to," snapped the judge.

"Time is money," said Doring. He looked at Jeff Miles, who was still smarting from the judge's rebuke. "Do something, you twit. What the hell am I paying you for?"

"Everyone on the porch," said the judge. "I'm going to say this once. This is a court of law. I am a judge. Respect this court and me, or I'll hold you in contempt. I don't like fancy objections, so don't bother me with 'em. I don't like cussing when I'm on the record so keep your tongues civil. For the record, this hearing is being held on Tuesday, August sixteenth on what is commonly known as Poor Farm Number Thirty-Eight."

He took a seat, then looked at me. "You first, Mr. Harrington."

I stood up, realizing for the first time that I was wearing blue jeans and a T-shirt sporting five mosquitoes and the caption "Bite Me."

"Under the Constitution, blacks were considered property. Slavery was a recognized institution. State courts and the U.S. Supreme Court recognized the supremacy of whites. In California, a court took as fact that people with yellow skin were an inferior race. No court in the country would make those pronouncements today because the rationale underpinning these decisions failed the test of reason, of science, and of time.

"Today, all races of people are entitled to basic human rights—the right, for example, to be free from bodily assault and from restraint. These rights are said to be inherent, not granted by the state. I'm asking this court to consider what we know about primates, about their mental awareness, of their ability to think, create, comprehend, feel pain, and suffer like humans, and to conclude that this entitles them to the same protection under the law as humans. The law should recognize them as persons and deal with assaults on their liberties as it would a human person of equal mental capacity."

Howard laughed derisively. "I don't care whether a chimp can paint the *Mona Lisa* or count or recite the Gettysburg Address. The chimp is *my* property. I paid for it, meaning I can do with it what I want. And I want it back *now*."

Judge McKenna pointed his finger at Jeff Miles, the DMI General Counsel. "You tell this man to keep quiet, or I'll find him in contempt. He can spend a few days in the slammer and see how *he* likes being locked up in a cage."

Miles seemed caught between his fear of Doring and his fear of the court's power.

"I'll defer to Mr. Doring, your Honor," I said. "Let him speak."

"As you wish," said the judge. "You want to vent, Mr. Doring, now's the time. But you'll shut up when I tell you to."

"I don't know what the hell is the matter with you people," said Doring. "The chimp is my property. A scientist who works for me was murdered and the chimp was stolen." Doring pointed at me. "He is in possession of stolen property and should be arrested as an accomplice to murder. Any fool can see that."

"Apparently not this fool," replied the judge. "I think Mr. Harrington is arguing that the chimp is not property, but has inalienable rights that this court should respect. What do you say to that?"

"It's crap!" barked Doring, pointing his cane at Judge McKenna. "Humans were made in the image of God. We won the evolutionary race because God wanted us to. But evolution hasn't stopped. We can and must do everything we can to survive. Killing a rabbit or a chimpanzee is meaningless in the battle for human survival. Anyone who says otherwise is either an idiot or a liar."

"Does that logic apply to retarded people?" I asked. I had read an article in which Doring had advocated testing on people with severe brain damage.

Doring smiled at me. "I have no reservations about testing on humans—the poor, the retarded, prisoners. I don't care. Nature used to take care of the weak and imperfect. Only our meddling has allowed these unfortunate creatures to sustain themselves. The lives of these people are worthless. I have no qualms about using them to advance science."

His words evoked an eerie silence. Even Doring's attorney looked away. Judge McKenna stared in disbelief. "I'm still not clear on your response to the contention that chimps are entitled to the same rights as humans under the Constitution," said McKenna.

Doring rolled his eyes. "As far as inalienable rights, that's liberal dogma. Rights don't fall from the sky. Rights are given by the powerful to the weak. Wrapping that truth in legal babble is just what lawyers do to justify their existence."

"So your argument," said the judge, "is that we are made in the image of God and have the right to torture creatures God made but not in His image? You believe that God has granted us a license to be cruel and uncaring? Do you believe the government has the right to do the same to you?"

Doring bristled, then poked Jeff Miles. "Answer him, you idiot."

Jeff stood, anger flashing in his eyes. "The point is, your Honor, that Mr. Harrington is asking you to name him the guardian of an animal, but there is no basis in the law to be named the legal guardian of property. Mr. Harrington can make all the principled arguments he wants. He cannot, however, change the legal precedent by concocting a legal fiction. Even this hearing cannot be justified under any supportable legal theory." Jeff held up a document that looked to be twenty pages long. "There is, however, ample case law to support DMI's property claim."

"What did he say?" asked Frieda.

Harvey whispered, "Shep has to come up with something solid. Otherwise, the court can't stop DMI from taking the chimp."

"That stinks," said Cecil.

Judge McKenna cleared his throat. "That seems to be the nub

of the issue."

Carrie appeared. Kikora was at her side. They stepped onto the deck. A collective "aw" rose from the small crowd. "Do you know that Kikora means hope in Swahili?" asked Carrie. "Isn't that the nub of the issue? Hope?"

Howard Doring turned toward Carrie. Suddenly, Kikora began screaming. She jumped on Carrie, almost knocking her down. I ran from the porch and took Kikora, who, though struggling, couldn't break free because of the drug I'd given her.

"I'll take that as testimony that Kikora doesn't want to leave," said Judge McKenna.

"All right, Shep. Convince me that I have the power to name you the legal guardian of a non-human."

I suddenly felt trapped. "There is no question that Kikora will be harmed if she is returned to DMI. That harm will come when she's injected with a potentially lethal dose of a diet drug that will destroy her liver and heart. I expect that an open-minded court will hear arguments in favor of person status for Kikora and grant me temporary custody of her while a suitable home is found." I held up my own stack of papers. "There is ample scientific data supporting the conclusion that chimpanzees have minds. I'm not an expert on chimpanzees, but I'm confident that at trial I can provide expert testimony and scientific data to support my contentions. Chimpanzees are individuals, aware of who they are, aware of..."

Judge McKenna held up his hand. "I didn't ask you that, Mr. Harrington. I asked if you could demonstrate that a court in Virginia was likely to agree with you." He held my gaze for a moment, then looked at Jeff Miles. "When will testing begin?"

Jeff glanced at Doring. "The schedule calls for the first dose of the drug to be administered to the test sample in two weeks."

"Okay," said the judge. "I'm holding you to that, Mr. Miles.

Today is the sixteenth. Don't be injecting anyone before the thirtieth, or I'll hold you and Mr. Doring in contempt." Judge McKenna looked at me. "Mr. Harrington, while I've taken care to see that no tests will take place for two weeks, I must tell you that to my way of thinking, you will have a difficult time in this state winning on the merits. I'm afraid I have no choice under the law but to return Kikora to DMI. My decision is made without prejudice should you choose to enlighten this court at a later date, say under a writ of habeas corpus supported by the kind of evidence you described. The motion for guardianship is denied, and this case is dismissed."

A man took Kikora from me and rushed her to a van parked behind the limo. Kikora began signing frantically. A moment later, I heard Carrie scream, then watched her move toward the back of the house.

"And what about him?" yelled Doring. "I want him arrested."

"The arrest warrant is vacated," said Judge McKenna.

"He's a thief," screamed Doring.

"And you're an ass," retorted the judge. "This court is adjourned."

Doring poked me with his cane. "You stay out of my business," he hissed.

I lunged for him, but Reggie restrained me. "Let it go, Mr. Harrington," he said.

Five minutes later, the DMI contingent left the farm and Kikora was gone.

"Shep?" said Judge McKenna. "I'd like a word with you in private."

I had a few things to say to the judge, none of them pleasant. We stepped inside the house, and I gave in to my frustration. "Why in God's name did you bother to come out here?" I demanded. "You could have saved her, but instead you sent her to die."

The judge glared back. "Is that what this is about? Saving you from guilt? You listen to me. Before you decide to pretend to be a lawyer again, I hope for your client's sake you are better prepared. I've heard law students make better arguments."

We stood facing each other, like two angry bulls ready to butt heads.

Finally, Judge McKenna shook his head. "You know I didn't mean that. I thought you did a good job. You just couldn't win. The question you face now is what to do with the time I gave you. If you want to see this through, you'll need to understand who the enemy is."

"Howard Doring," I said confidently.

The judge folded his arms across his chest. "Wrong, counselor."

"Then who?"

"Sit down," he commanded, "and I'll give you a history lesson."

I wasn't in the mood to be lectured to, but I didn't have the energy to say so.

We sat for a moment, the judge's eyes unfocused as he sorted his thoughts. "Like most older judges in this state," he said finally, "I was schooled in the doctrine of *stare decisis*. The law should be final, predictable, and determinative, even if this means that a decision is unfair. I adhered to this principle, issuing decisions that were unfair and that defied common sense, all to preserve the law. Then I heard a case brought by a man who, as a sixteen-year-old, had been sterilized against his will by a doctor at a state hospital. The procedure was legal. State law allowed for sterilization of the 'unfit'. After the procedure, this teenager turned eighteen, was drafted, and sent to fight the Nazis. Ironically, the Nazis were doing the same thing to the German population. Their program was based on the Virginia law and U.S. Supreme Court opinion that said the law was constitutional. What the Nazis took away from the Virginia model and our highest court was that experimenting on the 'unfit' was okay.

"When he returned home, the Virginia man wanted to resume a normal life, to live the American dream. What he wanted most was a family, but, of course, having been sterilized, he couldn't have one, except through adoption. He sued for compensation. Despite the U.S. Supreme Court case and a long line of state court opinions upholding the Virginia statute, I granted him a trial and let a jury award him damages. I couldn't imagine the law denying a remedy to a man who was by all accounts a war hero. My decision was overturned on appeal and remanded for a new trial before a new judge, who happened to be a strict constructionist. He and judges like him are your enemy and your client's enemy. The plaintiff lost the second trial, and the principle of *stare decisis* was preserved. My decision in that case killed my chances of being promoted to the court of appeals and the state supreme court, but I've been a better judge because of it."

"Kikora doesn't have a chance," I said, finally understanding the judge's point.

"You have to decide," answered Judge McKenna, "whether you want to pursue her case or not. In my opinion, it will take years and a lot of judges' funerals before new thinking will find its way into the legal system. Things have gotten better in the judiciary in recent years, but we have a long way to go yet."

"So why did you bother with a hearing?" I asked again.

"I was afraid if I didn't hold a hearing, you would do something stupid," he said. "Reilly pleaded with me to help you when you went to prison, but I was powerless to do anything. When I heard your story about the chimp, I realized I couldn't save your client, but I could save you, at least for the time being." Judge McKenna stood up and headed for the door. I followed him. "I admire your enthusiasm, Shep, but you're being naïve if you think the battle for chimps' rights will be an easy one. I'm not sure how I would rule given all the facts, but I doubt many judges would even listen. That doesn't mean you shouldn't try. But you have to be realistic."

Cali, with Frieda and Carrie beside her on the porch,

announced that the three ladies were going back to the house. "Are you going to be okay?" Cali asked me.

"Yeah. I'll be fine," I replied.

"Call me," she said, giving me a peck on the cheek before leaving.

I watched them drive off. The judge returned to his car and retrieved his fishing gear. "You remind me a lot of Reilly," he said. "I really miss him." He gave me a knowing look, then disappeared behind the house.

For a moment, I thought I was alone. Then I noticed the police cruiser still parked on the grass in front of the house. I spotted Detective Mason leaning against a nearby tree, his arms folded. He stepped out of the shade, and joined me on the porch.

"Shouldn't you be heading back to work?" I asked, not hiding my irritation.

"I *am* working," he said. "I'm keeping an eye on you to be sure you don't chase Howard Doring."

"Have fun," I said.

"You could at least offer me something to eat or drink," replied the detective. "That would be the hospitable thing to do."

I shook my head. "You know, I'm not in the mood to be hospitable. I'm not in the mood to be around anyone. So just sit in your cruiser and do what you have to do and leave me be."

He slipped off his hat. "If you get to feeling friendly, you let me know. I like to talk when I'm being treated friendly. I might even tell you a story about a murder, something that you might find real interesting."

I studied him for a moment. "Where are my manners, Detective? Would you care for a bite to eat?"

"I would," he replied, "and you can call me Reggie."

CHAPTER
ELEVEN

Reggie volunteered to fix lunch, and I agreed, my assignment limited to pointing out where I kept sandwich fixings and staying out of his way. Ten minutes later, Reggie, carrying two humongous sandwiches, lead me to the porch.

"Salami," I said without enthusiasm.

"You've never had a salami sandwich like this," he responded, anticipating my first bite.

My mouth full, I nodded in delight.

"The Salami Balami," he said. "Between two slabs of salami are tomatoes, Vidalia onion slices, cheese, and diced jalapeños, nuked in a microwave and laid on two slices of whole wheat smeared with Thousand Island dressing. It tastes better with beer, but I'm on duty."

While we ate, Reggie chatted away about growing up on a farm, attending a central high school, and dealing with white people. "I don't think you all are so different," he said. "You got your white racists. We got our black racists. It's stupid, but I guess it balances out. What gets me is educated white people like Howard Doring who actually believe that blacks are inferior to whites. That kind of attitude makes me think about kicking his white ass."

"Maybe when we aren't so busy, both of us together should kick his ass," I said. "You know, in the name of racial harmony."

Reggie gave me a broad grin. "Kind of a social bonding program. We could call it Ass-kicking for Humanity. I like that."

After we cleaned up the kitchen, we took a cooler of sodas to the porch and parked it between two chairs. I brought out all the munchies Kikora hadn't eaten and we sated ourselves on empty calories and fat. For a while, we listened to a summer symphony of cicadas, crickets, and birds. Reggie finished a soda, then grabbed another. "When you called and agreed to turn over the chimp, I figured you weren't ready to go back to prison," he said.

"Excuse me?" I said, surprised by the statement.

"I was just thinking about you sitting in prison for three years knowing you were innocent and no one believing you. That had to be hard. So when Harvey called and told me about the hearing, I was more than a bit surprised."

"Are you making a point, or accusing me of being a coward?"

"No offense intended," he said. "Just thinking out loud. I mean, you decided to fight DMI. But I'm sure it was a hard decision."

Intended or not, his comment irked me. "Maybe you think too much," I said.

Reggie took a handful of chips and jammed them into his mouth. He crunched loudly for a moment, then said, "I was thinking about Vail and Stone and how it was all for nothing."

"It?" I asked.

"It. The murder. Vail kills the doctor to save the chimp and all three of 'em lose."

"Not smart," I said curtly.

"Murder is never smart," said Reggie. "It may feel good, but it ain't smart." He picked at the tab on his soda can, making a twanging sound. "I like investigating murders. I know that sounds sick, but to me it's like putting together a puzzle. Mighty satisfying when all the pieces fit. I got the autopsy results last week but still don't have the toxicology results. Used to be that the autopsy and the tox report were important pieces of the puzzle, but DNA evidence changed all that. Celia Stone had skin under her fingernails. I found a few drops of blood on the carpet that didn't match the victim's blood type, so I sent a sample to a lab in Charlottesville for a DNA test. When Freeman fingered Sydney Vail as the killer, I got a warrant and searched Vail's house. I had the same lab run a DNA test on hair I found on a brush at Vail's house. The blood and skin were hers. Pretty cool, huh?"

"Makes her sound guilty," I said.

"It does," he said. "But it's odd that no other fingerprints or hair were found in the room where Stone died, not even Stone's. The only secretions we found other than Stone's belonged to Sydney Vail." He read my face. "I thought the same thing," he continued. "Should have been lots of fingerprints and hair. Someone cleaned up the prints and vacuumed the carpet, but left Sydney's blood and such behind. Someone also accessed Stone's laptop. We think some files were removed, but we don't know if that was before or after Stone was killed."

"Did you check the browser history, cache, and cookie files?" I asked.

"Wiped clean. The hard drive was defragmented, too," added Reggie.

The answer both puzzled and intrigued me. "And the murder weapon?"

"Haven't found that either," answered Reggie.

"So the popular wisdom is that Sydney killed Celia Stone, wiped the house clean of prints but left behind blood, took the time to check out Stone's computer, then left the house with a chimp and a murder weapon?"

Reggie swatted at an insect. "I know," he said. "Doesn't sound like a random act of violence, but it's too messy to be a professional killing. Too many loose ends."

I like order and hate disorder. What Reggie described made no sense to me, but only because the context that would give the facts order and logic was unknown. What remained to be seen was whether that context was knowable.

"I'm confused," I said. "Stone was killed by a blow to the head. Doesn't skin under the nails suggest a struggle?"

"Normally," answered Reggie.

"Were there signs of a struggle?" I asked.

Reggie gazed at the house. "No," he said. "Another loose end."

"One more question," I said. "You must have checked Vail's car for the victim's blood."

"We did," answered Reggie, "but we didn't find any."

"You'd think that if she removed the murder weapon, she'd leave some of Stone's blood behind somewhere."

Reggie wiped a bead of sweat from his face. "I'm a detective. I solve crimes by looking at evidence. Defense attorneys want to know what I know, but they don't want to tell the prosecutor or me what *they* know. Let's say that Sydney Vail has an explanation for everything I found. Her attorney will advise her not to answer any questions. So, I don't actually have all the facts. Personally, I can't draw a conclusion. Professionally, it's my job to do just that. So professionally I believe Vail's the killer because the best evidence I have points to her. Personally, I can't say I know for sure."

We were quiet for a moment, then Reggie said, "Think about what I've told you. Isn't there an obvious question that you'd like to ask me?"

"Come on, Reggie. I'm too tired to play games."

"Just think for a moment while I use your bathroom."

When he returned, I put the question to him this way: "Why was Stone keeping a chimpanzee at her house?"

Reggie smiled, then shrugged. "I don't know."

"The prosecution's case seems to be missing a few legs," I said.

"The story doesn't hang together," agreed Reggie, "but that

isn't going to help Sydney Vail. If she goes on trial for killing Celia Stone, minor inconsistencies in the evidence aren't going to help her. It's a political thing. People who live in Leaks County have a good thing going. Lots of people are making lots of money, and they know that the source of all that money is Stone's employer, Doring Medical Incorporated. The jury may not have any DMI employees on it, but I guarantee you that all members of the jury know that DMI is the goose that lays the golden eggs. I doubt they'll be sympathetic to any-one they perceive as a threat to DMI, and you know that's how the prosecutor will present Sydney Vail."

"So you're saying it's a hopeless case?" I asked.

Reggie shrugged. "You've got three problems. The evidence points to her as the killer. The odds are she *is* the killer. Worse, even if she isn't the killer, the jury will convict her anyway. And the investi-gation is closed, meaning that I'm not authorized to work other leads. In my view of the world, that adds up to hopeless. Unless, of course, someone on the outside finds the real killer."

"Yeah," I said, "why didn't I think of that?"

I walked him to his car. "Why did you decide to share this with me?"

Reggie stopped. "I like being a cop," he said softly. "I like to think my job is to find the truth and lock up the bad guys. This case is about politics, not the truth. The Commonwealth's Attorney is think-ing about running for office. DMI is telling him what to do and donat-ing a lot of money to his campaign. I want to catch whoever killed Stone and make 'em pay. I guess I don't believe Sydney did it, at least I'm not sure enough to put her in a cell and throw away the key just yet."

"I'm not sure where to begin," I said.

Reggie puffed out his cheeks. "Before we get to that, you gotta know one more thing—if you go around asking a lot of questions, you're asking for trouble. Howard Doring isn't a nice man. He's borrowed a lot of money from some not nice people. They don't like being messed with."

I laughed. "I love messing with those kind of people most of all."

"I knew you'd say that," said Reggie, tossing his hat on the seat and angling his huge frame into his cruiser. "Me too."

"Any suggestions on what I should do first?"

"Ask Sydney to think about what she saw when she went to the house," replied Reggie. "Details are important. Of course, you tell me what she says, and I'll use it against her. You also need to start with the victim and work backwards. Talk to anyone who knew her—her neighbors, her friends, her coworkers, her family. If you're lucky, you'll find a motive for killing her, and from that you can draw up a list of suspects." He handed me a newspaper. "Dr. Stone's body was released by the medical examiner a few weeks ago. Took a while for her family to claim it. Her obituary is on the last page. Funeral's tomorrow. If you decide to get involved in this, understand that it won't be easy and you're probably not going to succeed. I did a little investigating into Stone's background myself and she pissed off about everyone she ever met. Sorting through all those folks will take time, and I frankly doubt it'll produce a good suspect. Of course, if you decide not to get involved, Sydney Vail is toast and you'll never know whether you could have made a difference."

"What about you?" I asked.

"I can't do anything official or compromise the prosecutor's case against Sydney Vail. I'll pass on what I can, but you gotta be smart about this. I like you, but you can't come to Byron's Corner and expect I won't arrest you if you do something stupid."

"Thanks," I said.

"You watch your backside," he said, and drove away.

CHAPTER
TWELVE

At first, the possibility that Sydney Vail didn't kill Celia Stone buoyed my spirits. I could see her escaping the executioner, maybe even getting probation for stealing Kikora. I could see Howard Doring fuming over Sydney's liberation. Making Howard unhappy was a good thing. But the wind came out of my sails after I gave Harvey a play-by-play of my conversation with Reggie.

"Without proof that Sydney's story is true, without something to give to the jury besides conjecture and implication, the only thing your summation of the evidence can do is create false hope," he said. "Until you have something tangible, I want you to leave her defense to me."

I wasn't certain what I'd expected Harvey to say, but blowing me off wasn't on my list of possibilities. In retrospect, Harvey was right. I was coaching from the sidelines and avoiding contact. I sat on the porch swing and rocked slowly to the buzzing of insects, the chirping of birds, and the distant whining of truck tires on the interstate. A little more than two weeks ago, I had sat here drinking coffee, my day planned, my time committed. I had known nothing of chimpanzees or their plight. Even if I had some awareness that chimps were endangered, the problem wasn't mine to solve. Then Sydney and Kikora arrived and little by little changed my perspective on what was important. I had taken up their cause as best I could, fought a legal battle I couldn't win, and done more than could fairly have been expected of me. Any obligations I had to protect them had expired. I was free to return to my life as I knew it, to get on with my agenda, to do what I wanted to do.

I was free, but I didn't feel free.

I confess to a certain cynicism toward the criminal justice system. As a system created and operated by humans, the system is susceptible to error, arrogance, and abuse. But if I'd learned anything from the events of the morning, it's that the system can be affected by the best of human nature as well.

Detective Reggie Mason, a cop, charged with enforcing the law, had confessed to me his doubts about conclusions drawn from the evidence relating to Stone's murder. Judge McKenna, charged with determining what the law is and imposing punishment on its violators, confessed to me that the law is sometimes ignorant, valuing predictability over principle or common sense.

Both of these men were cogs in the justice machinery, and each had asked me to help him. Reggie, a black man whose experience with injustice I can't begin to imagine, saw the possibility of Sydney Vail's innocence, but could do nothing to stop her prosecution. Judge McKenna, who had seen the evil in treating legal precedent as God-like gospel and who had recognized the possibility that Kikora had certain inherent rights, fashioned a two-week stay of execution for Kikora so I might pursue a formal legal challenge to her incarceration.

I was free to resume my previous life only if I could live with the knowledge that I might have been able to help Sydney and Kikora and chose not to. This was the choice that Reggie and Judge McKenna had left on my doorstep. Complaining about injustice was easy. Doing something about it was a whole different ballgame.

I called Cali and asked her to meet me for coffee. Before she would let me hang up, I had to assure her I was all right. That discussion led her to question how I could possibly be all right under the circumstances. I extricated myself from the conversation by agreeing to meet in an hour at Java Java, a coffee boutique operated by Phil Brown, a friend and the owner of Brown's Chinese and American Café. I showered, then drove to my office. I checked my messages, rationalized that none of them was urgent, and headed to Lyle.

As always, most of the tables outside the Java Java coffee shop were full. The popularity of designer coffee in Lyle continues to amaze me. Lyle has a population of less than 4,000. While it is the county seat of Morgan County, a small splinter of land along Interstate 66, money is hard to come by and most people spend it carefully. Three dollars for a cup of coffee mixed with milk and chocolate syrup and whipped into an icy froth seems extravagant even to me. And yet, the Java Java does a brisk business seven days a week. I wondered if Phil might be doping the coffee with one of his favorite herbs.

I took a seat and waited for Cali. I recognized the faces of many of the patrons, but couldn't recall their names. Even so, eye contact was met with a nod of the head or quick wave of the hand.

Lyle is a town that likes to talk. Snippets of conversations swirled around me, and I eavesdropped like a native.

"...all she talks about. As if no one ever had a kidney stone."

"I heard Marvin's in a bad way. Prostrate trouble."

Silence.

"Pete's daughter just had a baby."

"Didn't she just have a baby last year?"

"Different father..."

I found this last bit of gossip titillating, but lost the thread when Cali appeared and sat down.

She scanned my face. "I thought you'd be pretty bummed out over what happened to Kikora," she said. "Instead, you have that same look I saw last Christmas."

A waitress took our order. I handed Cali the non-disclosure agreement that I had her sign earlier. "We don't need this any more," I said. "I appreciate all the help."

"What the hell is going on?" she said, wagging a finger at me.

"Nothing," I replied. "You've got your story. I think you should write it. I'm certain Bradley misses you."

"Why are you trying to get rid of me?" She stared into my eyes, then leaned back in her chair. "You haven't given up yet. You think Sydney Vail is innocent."

"How do you do that?" I demanded.

My question was answered with silence. The unstated answer was that Cali and I were soul mates, connected by some intangible link. Soul mates have few secrets from each other. Perhaps that's why they can only be around each other for brief periods of time.

"You're going to tell me eventually," she said. "May as well get it over with."

Our coffee arrived. I went through the facts as related by Reggie. Cali played with her hair as I detailed each inconsistency in evidence. When I was finished, she was smirking.

"What?" I said.

"You really get passionate about people who you think are being screwed by the system," she said.

"Well, I've been there."

Cali made a slurping sound with her straw. "You know I'm not just going to walk away from this," she said.

"Listen to me," I said, squeezing her hand. "I don't know who is involved in Stone's murder. I almost got you killed the last time I got involved in investigating a homicide. I'm not going to put you in harm's way again." She responded with a stare. "I'll e-mail you everything I learn. You can write the story as it unfolds."

"Do you think I blame you for what happened last Christmas?"

asked Cali. "Let's get something straight. I'm a reporter. I pursue stories because I choose to. I don't want you, or need you, to protect me. I'm a big girl. As for what happened at Christmas, I'm as much to blame as you, and I have to deal with my conscience from time to time just like you. The bottom line is that Sydney Vail will come to trial in a few months and DMI will begin testing on Kikora in two weeks. The trail is already cold. You don't have time to investigate Celia Stone by yourself. You need me."

Reluctantly, I agreed with her. "All right. You go back to Byron's Corner and ferret out everything you can about Celia Stone's social life. You mentioned that Celia fired a lab tech—Henry Thomas—and some guy she had a fling with."

"Devon," said Cali.

"Gus can do background checks on anyone you want," I continued. "But if things get hot, you're going to go home."

"What are you going to do?"

"I'm going to a funeral," I replied, "and see what the living have to say about the dead."

With a plan in place, we drank our coffee in a silence that at first seemed comfortable and familiar. But as time passed, Cali seemed more preoccupied. Glancing at me intermittently, she finally said, "We need to talk." Despite the heat, her serious tone sent a chill down my spine.

"We are talking," I replied lamely, hoping to avoid whatever topic she had in mind.

"We need to talk about you, me, and Bradley," she said forcefully.

I nodded but was unable to look at her. I had known that one day we'd be having this discussion about us (although Bradley had not figured into my thinking). Its inevitability didn't make it any easier.

Cali squeezed my hand. "He's asked me to marry him."

I digested this piece of data anticipating an angst-filled reaction. To my surprise, mixing with a multitude of other emotions was a feeling of relief, although I couldn't explain why. Unable to formulate a meaningful response, I ran for safe ground. "Congratulations," I said, trying to sound sincere. "That's really very exciting news."

A deepening furrow crossed Cali's forehead. She glared back at me disapprovingly. *"Exciting,"* she said evenly. "Really? You think Bradley's proposal is exciting?"

"Not anymore." I struggled in the face of her punishing stare. "What I meant was that Brad is an inconsiderate jerk and should be punished severely for putting you in a terribly awkward position."

Cali finished her coffee and stood up. "You're very tired," she said. "We'll talk about this after you've had some sleep and can think rationally."

She gave me a "it's not your fault—you're male" look and walked away.

I walked to my office a bit dazed. I had no idea what response would have satisfied Cali, nor did I have the energy to think about it. I thought about other things, my attention hopping from one idea to another thanks to a good caffeine buzz.

The moment I stepped inside, Van Gogh jumped up on my desk, gave me an annoyed look, butted my chin with the top of his head, and purred loudly. I went to the kitchen and opened a can of tuna for him and a soda for me, then found the newspaper Reggie gave me and flipped through it looking for Celia Stone's obituary. After coffee with Cali, I figured I might relate better to the dead than to the living.

The article identified her survivors as an older sister named Darla and a younger sister named Melissa. Her funeral was to be held in Kale, Pennsylvania the next morning. The article went into some

detail about Celia's accomplishments as a DMI scientist, her educa-
tion, and how she was allegedly "brutally slain" in her own home by
Sydney Vail, "a known militant animal rights activist." The obituary
writer apparently had read the story in the Byron's Corner paper and
accepted it as fact.

After reading the article several times, I was struck by how little it really told about Celia Stone's life. Drawing conclusions from
what isn't said is a risky exercise, but my hunch was that there was little to tell. Stone had never married. She wasn't going to be buried in
Byron's Corner, which suggested she hadn't put down roots there. I
surmised that because she worked long hours, she had few hobbies or
interests, or little time for social activities. Her life was her work. In
my sketch of her, she was a loner, and yet she felt enough for a chimpanzee to die protecting it. Why was that? Maybe I would learn the
answer to that question at her funeral.

The tinkling of bells at the front door pulled me from Celia
Stone's obituary. I looked up to see Robbie leaning against the doorjamb. "You look like hell," she said. "I heard things didn't go well this
morning."

"I lost the case, and my client, a chimp, didn't pay me," I said.
"Not a good beginning."

"Why do I get the feeling you're not done yet?"

I rubbed my eyes. "Do you have Theo Levitz's number?"

"And why would you want to talk to a constitutional lawyer?"
asked Robbie.

I stood up. "Because I want to file a motion for habeas corpus
in Federal District Court on behalf of Kikora alleging violation of her
rights under the Thirteenth Amendment of the U.S. Constitution. And
because Theo is crazy enough to help me do it."

I escorted Robbie to her office. "You don't know anything

about a pile of feathers behind my desk, do you?" she asked.

"Gee, no. Wait, I remember now. I hurled them there and forgot to clean them up."

"I don't mind giving Van Gogh a place to sleep," she said angrily, "but I don't want him dragging dead things into my office and eating them."

"I'll have a talk with him," I replied. "He should eat in the kitchen like everyone else."

Robbie took a seat and began flipping through her Rolodex. "I remember you saying something about pissing off Theo when you were in law school."

"I worked on a human rights project for him my third year," I replied. "He wanted me to pursue the research after I graduated, but I found business and technology more interesting. I don't think he's still holding a grudge. I saw him at my trial, and I know he consulted with my defense attorneys while I was in prison."

She wrote down the number. "One more thing," I said. "I'm going to need you to watch over my clients. I'll take care of the major problems, but if you could make excuses for me with the rest, that would be great."

"How long will you be out?" asked Robbie.

I thought about Gus's offer of employment. "I don't know," I said. "Two weeks."

"If I can help in any way, you know I will," said Robbie.

I thanked her and went back to my office. I left a message for Theo, then called Jerome, the primate authority I'd met at the zoo. I expected to get his answering machine, but he answered on the second ring. "I get Tuesday afternoons off," he said. I offered to take him to dinner, but he countered with dinner at his house. "I like what I cook because I know what's in it, and it's cheaper," he said.

I went home to pack a dark suit for the funeral and to get a fresh battery for my cell phone. I wanted to beat the rush hour traffic around Washington, but exhaustion caught up with me. I set my alarm and fell asleep thinking about Sydney and Kikora, and wondering what would become of them.

CHAPTER
THIRTEEN

Jerome lived in a nice house in Bethesda, Maryland just over the D.C. line. His brick residence, which was painted white, had dark blue shutters and a slate roof. A manicured lawn, crisply trimmed boxwoods, and perfectly shaped trees looked to be the work of well-paid gardeners, not an aging homeowner.

I rang the doorbell and was greeted by a young woman who looked at me with sultry blue eyes. She wasn't smiling, but the softness of her features made it seem that way. She was wearing khaki slacks and sandals. A black sleeveless top, cut at the midriff, accentuated her curves and firm abs. "You must be Shep Harrington," she said gesturing me inside. "My father told me about you."

She spoke softly, but her eyes beamed with confidence. "Jerome is your father?" I asked.

She brightened at the question. "He says he is," she replied as she led me through the living room to a patio in the back of the house.

Jerome stood. "I see you've met my daughter, Heather. When you see us together, it either casts doubt on genetic theory or suggests my wife was dabbling in someone else's genetic pool." He laughed and kissed her on the forehead. "Heather's mother was from Thailand. That's were she gets her dark eyes and bronze coloring. What she gets from me has yet to be determined." He laughed, then added, "Heather is a behavioral psychologist and has learned to put up with me. She occasionally works with primates who have been rescued from test labs. She's single, if you're wondering."

I was.

Heather gave her father a stern look, then turned her gaze back to me. For a moment, our eyes met, and I know I was sweating pheromones. Worse, I suspected Heather, as a behavior expert, knew it. "May I get you something?" she asked. "My dad and I are vegetarians. I hope you don't mind."

"Not at all," I said. "A beer would be fine."

She glided from the patio and Jerome motioned for me to sit down. "Having her father live with Heather can't do much for her social life, but she doesn't seem to care. So, I heard you rattled old Howard Doring's cage. I also heard that the chimp went back to DMI. You didn't have such a good day."

"No, sir," I replied, "but I prefer to think I've lost a battle, not a war. I need your help."

Heather returned with two frosted mugs of beer.

"And what war are you thinking of waging?" asked Heather.

She sat opposite me, her gaze intense. I couldn't shake the feeling she was studying me, and I found it distracting.

"One with two fronts," I replied, directing my answer to Jerome. "I'm not convinced that Sydney Vail murdered Celia Stone, but I need tangible evidence to prove it. I need to learn everything I can about Celia in hopes of finding someone with a reason to kill her."

"And the other front?" asked Heather.

"I'm going to try to protect Kikora by bringing a legal action on her behalf in federal court," I said.

"I'm intrigued," said Heather. "What would a court do to protect a chimpanzee?" she asked in a tone dripping with sarcasm.

"Maybe we should be pleasant rather than verbally abuse our guest," said Jerome. He looked at me. "Heather doesn't have a high opinion of lawyers, or judges for that matter, but it isn't personal."

An understated smile crept onto Heather's face. "No offense intended," she said. "But I'd like an answer."

"The action I'm considering would declare that chimpanzees are entitled to the basic rights granted by the Constitution," I replied.

"Why don't we eat dinner," said Jerome, "and talk about this later?"

"Dinner's not ready," countered Heather, "and I want to hear more about this. Are you going to argue chimps are human?"

I shook my head. "I don't want to bore you with legalese, and I'm no expert in constitutional law," I said, "but the gist of the argument is that we humans claim that certain rights are inherent—like the right to move freely and the right to control our bodies and minds. Our claim to these rights is largely based on the fact that normal human adults are in charge of their existence and can make decisions about what to do and what not to do. The law refers to this state as autonomy. The law grants these rights to human children and to the mentally challenged through various legal fictions even though the people in question are not fully autonomous. I want a court to rule that under the constitutional principle of equality, all living things should be entitled to these same inherent rights based on the standards we apply to ourselves.

"What I've read about chimps and other primates is that their mental abilities exceed those of most children. If children are entitled to protection from incarceration, kidnapping, vivisection, and whatever, then so are chimpanzees. I'll need to convince a court that chimpanzees have minds and that they are at least as autonomous as children. It won't be easy."

"Would you like my help?" asked Heather. "I've worked on a number of cognitive studies of chimpanzees and orangutans."

I felt as if I'd just won the lottery. "That would be great," I said, enjoying the prospect of seeing Heather again.

An electronic timer beeped from inside the house. "We can discuss the murder of Celia Stone after we eat," said Heather, standing up.

"Something to look forward to," added Jerome.

Dinner was salad and a tofu vegetable casserole seasoned with garlic and pepper. Both Heather and Jerome ate quickly, leaving me to eat and try to answer questions about my family and myself. Heather was more curious about my stay in prison than I was interested in talking about it, but she pursued the subject with clinical persistence until her father came to my rescue. "Let's have coffee on the patio," he said, and the inquisition ended.

The evening was cool and clear, the August humidity receding in the wake of an atypical cold front. I followed Heather to the patio while Jerome made coffee. "I didn't mean to pry," she said, sitting in a swinging chair. "I have been studying the behavior of chimpanzees recently released from lab cages and thought there might be something to learn from your experience. I sometimes forget the pain that comes from dredging up old memories."

"How do you insulate yourself from the cruelty we inflict on chimpanzees?" I asked.

She pursed her lips. "I don't. I cry and scream and get it out of my system."

Jerome arrived with coffee and a plate of brownies. "I have a sweet tooth," he confessed. "Can't have coffee without chocolate." He handed me a mug and a brownie. "I think it's time you get what you came for," he said. "Unfortunately, I don't know very much. Just rumors and stories I heard through the grapevine."

"What does the grapevine tell you about Celia Stone?" I asked.

Jerome consumed one brownie and took another. "Celia, like most perfectionists, was an autocrat. She was hell to work for, had a temper, and blamed others for her shortcomings and failures."

I snagged a brownie. "So why would she take care of a chimpanzee at her house?"

"Most people reach a point in their lives where they take stock," answered Heather. "The exercise can be traumatic for some, leading to all kinds of emotional responses. Celia was past her child-bearing years and not married. With her future looking like her past—work and more work—it wouldn't surprise me if the chimp stirred her nurturing instincts. Most primatologists are female because females tend to be better at picking up on the non-verbal cues of babies. The infant chimpanzee could have penetrated Celia's well-honed defenses, but then I'm just speculating."

"So," I said, "you're saying they bonded?"

"Yes," laughed Heather, "that would be the short-winded version."

I considered Sydney's story, reciting it briefly: "Sydney Vail is accused of killing Stone in a fight over Kikora. Sydney says that Stone asked her to take Kikora and to protect her. How does the bond between Stone and Kikora play into that story?"

Heather nodded. "With Celia's penchant for control, the bond, once made, would be very strong. Extrapolating from our profile of Stone, I'd say that Celia would fight anyone trying to take Kikora from her, but might give Kikora to someone if Stone believed she couldn't protect Kikora otherwise. Actually, the likelihood that Stone could keep DMI from testing on Kikora seems pretty remote, so I could see Stone surrendering Kikora to Vail, assuming, of course, she trusted Vail."

Jerome clasped his hands together. "I'm not sure this is relevant, but I've heard rumors about Celia seeking out male partners at conferences. I have no reason to believe them."

Heather raised her eyebrows and said to Jerome, "Perhaps the gentleman doth protest too much."

Jerome laughed, spilling his coffee. "She wasn't my type, and if she were, your mother would turn over in her grave."

"I hadn't thought of Celia as a party woman," I said.

"Sometimes control addicts let their hair down," said Heather. "Actually, having sex in a professional setting can be a manifestation of control. Choosing the partner is an act of dominance, and the sex is detached and purely about gratification. Seeking out multiple partners is also a way of diminishing the value of all the partners. The rumors that follow are met with indifference, again satisfying the need for control. If I'm correctly describing Celia Stone, then she was likely to be confused and erratic in her behavior."

"People like that make enemies," I said.

"They do," agreed Heather. "Whether any of them are prone to violence is another matter. Only a small fraction of the population actually assaults another person. Your murderer will be someone who is violent by nature or someone whom Celia pushed over the brink. Finding the killer sounds like a daunting task to me."

We sat silently for a moment, then Jerome leaned forward in his chair. "I don't know how to express this to you without sounding like an alarmist, but I would be remiss if I didn't mention it to you. Howard Doring, the head of DMI, is a very bad businessman. Over the years, he has lost a lot of money lent him by investors. His luck seemed to change with Doring Medical Incorporated. Mind you, DMI didn't actually research anything. Rather, Doring bought drug patents a few years before their expiration date, then licensed generics to drug makers. He was doing well until a patent infringement case almost bankrupted him. He cut a deal with a group of investors who are rumored to have connections to organized crime. After that, DMI survived and even went on an acquisition campaign. I've heard stories that companies refusing to deal with DMI on its terms suffered accidents—fires, lost data, even personal injuries to key employees. I'm telling you this to remind you to be discreet about who you talk to and what questions you ask."

I thanked him for his concern, and the conversation turned to social pleasantries—how good dinner tasted, why chocolate is good for you, and the weather. Half an hour later, I made a polite goodnight speech. Jerome opted to finish his coffee outside, leaving Heather to walk me to the door. "I have a videotape of chimps being held in small cages in test labs," she said. "I'll make you a copy if you think it could help you in your legal case."

"Thank you," I said. "Let me write down my address."

Heather looked at me with her flat smile. "No need," she said softly, her gaze lingering for a moment. "I'll find you."

CHAPTER
FOURTEEN

It was after 9 p.m. when I left Bethesda. I wasn't sleepy, so I took Rockville Pike, eventually found my way to Interstate 70, and headed north toward Pennsylvania and Celia Stone's funeral. Along the way, I checked my voice messages. Cali had dinner with some "interesting people with interesting things to say." Theo Levitz, my choice for Kikora's trial counsel, was out of town and not expected back until Thursday.

I began nodding off just before Hagerstown, Maryland. I found a chain motel and paid almost a hundred dollars for a room that wasn't much bigger than the one the feds gave me for free. Sleep came quickly, my dreams visited by Celia Stone, Cali, and Heather.

I've been to enough funerals to know that you can learn a lot about the deceased by observing the people who come to the services. I arrived at the church early and sat in the back so I could hear the conversations of the mourners before the occasion became quiet and solemn. My first observation was that there was no coffin, meaning the deceased had been cremated. Because the body had been released from the medical examiner weeks earlier, there had been more than ample time for a casket and even a wake, but no one had bothered. While there were other possible explanations, I surmised that the family wanted Dr. Stone's remains to be cremated and her ashes delivered by Federal Express to Kale, Pennsylvania. This conclusion left me feeling sorry for Celia Stone, though I'm not sure why.

The locals arrived and the church hummed with whispered conversations. I heard about a local high school football team's chances this fall, about someone who had a hip replaced, and about the new minister at the Lutheran church. I didn't overhear anyone lamenting the passing of Celia Stone. When two middle-aged women strolled up the aisle and sat in the front pew, heads turned. I assumed these were the sisters, Melissa and Darla, referred to in Stone's obituary. The minister gave the congregation the look that meant it was time to get down to the business of officially sending Dr. Stone to the Hereafter, and a polite quiet settled over the small gathering.

The minister talked about beginning as dust and returning to dust, which sort of made sense to me, then closed by saying that God loves all of his children and would welcome Celia home with open arms. I found the sentiment surprisingly moving and comforting. He then called on Melissa to say a few words. She rose from the front row and came to the lectern. She was attractive, but her eyes were too far apart to say she was pretty. She told a few amusing anecdotes about Dr. Stone's childhood fascination with microscopes and dead animals she'd found in the woods. Melissa struggled to say the right things, but she seemed to be talking about a stranger, not her dearly departed sister.

The second woman, whom the minister addressed as Darla, was on the bony side, her dark hair and gaunt face making her appear older than she was. But unlike Melissa, Darla mopped her eyes and spoke softly and reverently, and occasionally with a catch in her voice. I am cynical by nature, but I just didn't buy the act. Darla seemed to be playing the part of the victim, expressing her dismay that her sister had been "stolen" from her. When I looked around the congregation, no one else seemed to be buying the story either.

The minister blessed the ashes and said a prayer, then invited the congregation to meet in the reception hall to celebrate the life of Celia Stone.

The reception hall was in the church basement. I milled about, waiting for an opportunity to speak with Darla or Melissa. Darla was making the rounds, seeking solace for her real, or imaginary, loss. Melissa seemed to be doing her best to leave. I saw her shake hands with the minister, then exit by a side door, a pack of cigarettes in her hand. I followed her out and found her in a classic smoker's pose: elbow in hand, cigarette between thumb and index finger, head elevated, exhaling a plume of smoke. I bet myself she'd spit a tobacco flake, and won.

When Melissa noticed me, she gave me a hard look. "I'd like to be alone," she said.

"Darla seems to enjoy company," I replied, offering my hand. "I'm Shep Harrington. I'm sorry about your sister."

Melissa rolled her eyes. "Darla is a hypocrite. She hasn't spoken to Celia in ten years."

"Any particular reason?"

Melissa shot me a bitter smile. "Ten years ago, Darla found Christ. She became very judgmental to say the least. According to Darla, Celia's position on abortion and fetal research was immoral, as was Celia's association with men." Melissa shook her head. "That's Darla. She's had three husbands and a dozen boyfriends, and suddenly she takes the high road and passes judgment on the whole fucking world."

"Finding Christ sounds a lot like filing for bankruptcy," I said. "You forget about all your old debts and creditors and move on to new ones."

Melissa flicked the ash off her cigarette. "I guess."

"I thought you did pretty well, under the circumstances," I said.

"What circumstances?"

"Having to say something about someone when you didn't mean it. I've done it a few times myself and it's no fun."

She offered me a cigarette, but I declined. "I didn't say what I felt, mister, because what we did to Celia can't be changed."

I looked in Melissa's eyes and realized I'd misjudged her.

"Mom and Dad wanted a boy," said Melissa, her lip trembling. "Celia was a scrawny, weak little girl. She needed glasses and corrective shoes. Darla and I didn't get new bikes or new clothes because all the fun money went to take care of Celia." Melissa took a long drag from her cigarette and let it out slowly. "She tried to make us like her. We'd play with her, but then leave her locked in a closet or tied to a bed. She tried harder. She got the best grades, and won awards, but my father didn't care. Mom tried to be supportive, but she took a job and was too tired. Funny, though. When Celia turned twelve, she stopped asking us to play with her. She didn't even eat dinner with us. When she graduated high school, we didn't even know she was second in her class and had won a scholarship to MIT. Three days later, she left home without so much as a goodbye." Melissa shrugged. "What should I have said about my sister? She deserved better?"

She reflected for a moment, regained her composure, then asked, "How did you know her?"

"I didn't," I said. "The person who they say killed her is a friend of mine. I don't think she did it. I need to prove it."

"You're working for her killer?" asked Melissa, her voice strained. "Get the hell out of here."

"Your sister's killer is still out there," I said. "I need your help finding out who it is."

"Leave me alone," she said, lighting another cigarette.

"Okay," I said. "Oh, by the way, I liked your speech about Celia deserving better. I actually thought you meant it."

I'd taken a dozen steps when I heard her running toward me. "You asshole," she screamed. I turned, and she slammed her fist into my shoulder. Tears streamed down her cheeks. "Damn you. Damn you." Then she pressed her face into my shoulder and sobbed.

"I'm sorry," I said.

A few minutes later, her guilt spent for the moment, Melissa pulled back. "Thank you," she said. "I didn't mean…"

I patted her cheeks with a tissue. "Don't worry about it. I'm an attorney. The first billable hour is free. So is lunch, if you'd like."

"Just get me out of here," she said.

Melissa directed me to a small restaurant located in what looked like an old post office. The outside was marked with a generic "café" sign, but the inside smelled of fresh garlic, pasta, and coffee. Melissa declined to eat, ordering only a glass of wine. I ordered cappuccino and tiramisu. I went through the now familiar story of how Celia had been killed and the evidence that pointed to Sydney. I then summarized the many contradictions in the evidence. Melissa listened calmly, reacting only when I forgot to whom I was speaking and spoke more graphically than intended about the head injury that killed her sister.

"I used to watch Sydney Vail on TV," said Melissa. "She was very pretty."

I nodded. "Did Celia have any enemies—old boyfriends, business partners, jealous wives?" I asked.

"To be honest, I had only spoken to Celia a half dozen times in the last few years. Then, one day in June, she called me. After that, we spoke a few times a week until she was killed. I don't think she had boyfriends, not the usual way you mean. From what she told me, she didn't have any friends at all. Her neighbors hated her. Everyone who worked for her hated her. She didn't care much for men, except Devon Sheen, and that ended about two years ago. Last I heard, he was in prison."

Devon was the lowlife Cali had mentioned at lunch in Byron's Corner.

"Tell me about Devon," I said.

"Poor Celia," replied Melissa, shaking her head. "She finally met someone she liked. Out of nowhere I get this call from her telling me she might be bringing someone home to meet me. Devon was a smooth, handsome man who filled her head with romantic notions. Celia was in her fifties, and she was talking like a teenager. She met him at a conference and was swept off her feet. They spent time at some of the best hotels on the east coast. When Celia told me that she was paying for most of this, I told her straight out that Devon was up to something. She got mad, of course, said something about Devon's funds being tied up in notes, and advised me to mind my own business. Then she stopped calling me. A month later, a police officer called and started asking questions about Celia and Devon. Two months after that, Devon was arrested. Celia had caught on and turned him in. She wouldn't talk about him or how she figured it out, but she did say he'd pinned her to the wall and told her if she testified, he'd come back and slit her throat."

"Do you mind telling me what else you talked about recently?"

Melissa shot me a look that was all salt. "Yes, I do. Very much." The tears ran down her cheeks. "I guess I'm going to tell you anyway," she said drying her face on a napkin. "When Celia called in June, she said she'd suddenly awakened to the fact that she was in her mid-fifties and had no family other than Darla and me. No children. Nothing but her professional work."

"But she had Kikora," I said gently.

"I wasn't very empathetic," said Melissa, nodding, "but I listened anyway. Being around that chimp changed Celia. When she spoke about Kikora, it was in a maternal way. She had no idea that she was talking as if Kikora were her child. When I asked her how she could intentionally risk Kikora's life for a diet drug, Celia cried and said she didn't know. Her life was a mess right to the end."

"Was she having doubts about testing on chimps?" I asked.

Melissa shrugged. "She was confused, but I couldn't tell you what she was thinking."

The waitress arrived with our check. "Did Celia send you e-mail?"

"Sometimes," said Melissa. "Mostly just to see if I was at home so she could know when to call me."

"From work or from home?"

Melissa laughed. "She never e-mailed me from work because she thought the mail was monitored. She used a Yahoo! account. Her address was doctorock@yahoo.com."

I tossed a twenty on the table. "I guess you don't know her password?"

Melissa shook her head. "What is your mother's maiden name?" I asked.

"Poppavitch. Why?"

"Sometimes it helps when checking on people," I said. "It would also be helpful if you could make a list of the names of pets, people, dolls, anything that Celia might have used as a password. Oh, and one more thing. I'd like to visit Celia's house in Byron's Corner. I just need you to give me permission. If we could stop by your bank, they can type up a permission slip and notarize it."

Melissa scanned my face. "You'll tell me who really killed my sister?"

I nodded.

"Even if it's Sydney Vail?"

I said yes, but I didn't sound convincing, even to myself.

CHAPTER
FIFTEEN

I dropped off Melissa at the church and agreed to keep her apprised of developments in the murder investigation. On the way home, I called Cali. Between a half-dozen disconnects, I managed to understand that she'd located Henry Thomas in Staunton, the employee who had threatened Celia Stone after she fired him from DMI. I said that I was planning on meeting Theo in Charlottesville on Thursday and could join her in Staunton in the afternoon.

After a little meaningless chit-chat, she said, "You sound like you heard the dog died."

"Sorry," I responded. "I spent the day rooting around in the muck of what was Celia's life. I want to feel sorry for her, but, to be honest, I don't have a lot of sympathy for people who realize after fifty years that they've wasted their life. Sydney may be a fruit cake, but at least she's a fighter."

Cali seemed to agree. "Based on the conversations I've had with people who knew Celia," said Cali, "she irritated almost everyone she met."

I was about to agree with her when the connection died again. When the signal improved, I confirmed my appointment with Theo for 10:30 the next morning in Charlottesville, then settled back for the long drive home.

Stopping by my office, I changed into shorts and a T-shirt and checked my messages. Every client thinks his problem is urgent, so deciding which calls required immediate attention and which could wait was a complicated process. I made a small list of calls to return on my morning drive to Charlottesville, then noticed a package in my inbox. A yellow sticky included a note in Robbie's handwriting: "A woman named Heather dropped this by. Said she would come back tonight. I didn't watch it. Hope she didn't show it to her husband first. Robbie."

I went to Robbie's office and slid the tape into the VCR. The screen flashed colored confetti for a moment, then went black. The words "New York College of Technology - March 1998" popped onto the screen. Suddenly, and without any warning, I was bombarded with the screams of animals. It took me a minute to realize that the screams were coming from a honeycomb of small cages stacked on top of each other. The images moved erratically as the person shooting the scene walked hurriedly toward the end of the row. The perspective changed to inside one of the cages, where a chimpanzee was bent over, his eyes stony and unresponsive. Large patches of this chimp's fur were missing and blood oozed from several fingers. I had read about such conditions, but the video made it real—too real, actually.

I averted my eyes, but the narrator's somber, melodic voice pulled me back. "What you have seen is not uncommon."

The video made me angry and wary. Angry because I wanted to deny that humans could be so cruel to other living things, and wary because I didn't know whether to accept the narrator's statements at face value.

For a moment, the white-lettered words "Carlo's Story" appeared on the screen against a black background. Then the face of a chimpanzee appeared. "This is Carlo," said the disembodied voice. "Carlo was born in 1959. He has been in research since he was two.

He has been anesthetized—what researchers call being 'knocked down'—more than three hundred times. He has endured over fifty punch liver biopsies, a dozen wedge liver biopsies, bone marrow transplants, lymph node biopsies, and several infusions of HIV. While no important scientific data was obtained from Carlo, he has become anxious, aggressive, and fearful. During one fit of anxiety, he bit off his right index finger. Left to awake alone from knockdowns, he chewed off both his thumbs. During his last knockdown, a half dozen men shot darts into his body, while Carlo slammed himself into the bars of his cage. Sadly, he could live another ten years."

The camera focused on the eyes of this broken chimp, then faded to another black screen. The white letters, plain and emotionally neutral, warned that Sheila's story was next. A moment later, a picture of a chimp huddled in the corner of a small cage appeared on the screen. "Sheila won't show herself," said the narrator. "A family raised her as a pet in Florida. There she enjoyed bubble baths and wearing frilly dresses. Before she was three, she was brought to a lab, where she was involved in three studies involving forty liver biopsies. Like Carlo, her life in confinement caused her to suffer repeatedly from anxiety attacks. She, too, mutilated herself. At six-years-old, Sheila may have forty-five more years to live."

I watched the stories of five more chimpanzees, then turned off the tape. I sat in Robbie's chair and stared at the dark television screen, sorting through my emotions, trying to find an intellectual handhold to grab—one that would pull me safely away from the sheer cruelty depicted on the tape. I manufactured doubts about the authenticity of the scenes depicted in the tape by reminding myself that they could easily have been staged. I didn't want to believe that what I had just seen was the norm. Worse, if what I had seen was real, then Kikora's fate seemed even more hopeless. Surely the scientists who test on these unfortunate animals had heard the shrill voices of animal advocates a thousand times. I had nothing new to offer, no epiphany of moral insight that would change minds. Even Lincoln couldn't convince slave owners that holding humans in bondage was immoral. It took a bloody civil war to end slavery. No one was going to fight a war to save chimpanzees or other primates.

The ringing of the phone startled me, and I fumbled the receiver before answering. It was Sheriff Belamy. "You coming to bowl or should we get a substitute?"

I had almost forgotten that Wednesday was league night at the Bowlarama. In many towns, bowling isn't a big summertime sport, but Lyle's air-conditioned Bowlarama offered a perfect way to kill a hot August night in cool comfort. I wasn't in a socializing mood, but I knew better than to sit in my office alone with my thoughts. "I'll be there in a minute," I said, then hung up the phone. Maybe bowling was just what I needed.

Ten minutes later, I was retrieving my ball and shoes from my locker at the Bowlarama when Doc Adams, the Reverend Billy Trip, and Sheriff Belamy appeared.

"Hey, Shep," said Billy.

I was sixteen when the Reverend Billy Tripp arrived in Lyle. Although I didn't know it at the time, he wasn't actually a preacher but a forty-year-old paroled felon whose most refined skills were drinking and bowling. Somehow, he got off the bus and was confused for the replacement minister of the town's church. Billy learned on the job. His first sermon mixed doing God's work with throwing a good hook on an oily lane. But Billy was a voracious reader and he soon took on the task of leading the people of Lyle and Morgan County from wickedness.

"Good to see you, Reverend," I said.

"Evening, Shep," offered the sheriff.

Sheriff Belamy is one of the few cops I respect. A chunky man in his mid-sixties, he's both fair and honest, qualities that are over-shadowed by a long thin nose and deep-set eyes that give him a sinister look. Belamy has lived in Lyle for as long as I can remember, but I know little of his personal life. Even so, I like him. He's a good bowler and could be better if he worked on his consistency.

"Evening," I responded.

"We can stand around sounding like the Walton's," said Doc, "or we can say what we came to say while I'm still breathing."

Doc is as old as time. Cantankerous, moody, and sometimes brutally honest, he can be a serious nuisance. But when his mind is working on all cylinders, he's as smart and cunning as a fox. He doesn't bowl, but he likes to tell people what's wrong with their form.

Doc's request hung in the air for a moment. Sheriff Belamy cleared his throat and said, "Billy and I were talking to Garry Parsons and he was saying something about a police cruiser and a lot of limos showing up yesterday morning at the poor farm. We were just making sure you wasn't in any kind of trouble."

"Garry Parsons should be minding his own business," said Doc, who then looked at me. "So what kind of trouble are you in now?"

I gave a brief description of my first encounter with Sydney Vail, caring for Kikora, Sydney's confession, and the court hearing. When I was done, Doc, Billy, and Sheriff Belamy stood silently.

Doc broke the silence. "Do you attract trouble or do you go looking for it?"

"Sounds like this Vail lady has a mountain of trouble herself," offered the sheriff.

"Maybe. There's some question about whether Sydney actually killed Dr. Stone," I said. "I'm looking into a few loose ends."

Doc rubbed his chin. Billy looked at the floor. Sheriff Belamy groaned softly. "You sure you want to get involved with a situation like this?" asked the sheriff.

"I'm thinking the same thing," said Billy. "What we're getting at is that you're not a trained investigator. We understand that you want justice done. We just don't want anything to happen to you."

"Thanks. I appreciate your concern," I replied.

"Hell," said Doc, "Shep's got a nose like a bloodhound. He just has to shoot a bit sooner than he did the last time."

"I'll keep that in mind," I said.

I took my gear to a table and sat down. As I put on my shoes, I watched Billy warm up. For several weeks, he'd been having a miserable time on the lanes and tonight was no exception. I felt bad for him, especially given the effort he put into the game. Last week Billy called me to the church to witness a miracle. Thinking water-to-wine or attorney-to-saint, I went to church with great expectations. I called for Billy, but there was no answer. I took the stairs down to Billy's office, but he wasn't there. Then I heard a noise coming from the hallway and found Billy in the laundry room.

"Hey, Shep," he said, glancing at me before returning his attention to the sink. "You're just in time."

I joined him and peered into the tub. I saw a drywall bucket filled with a frothy liquid that barely covered a bowling ball. "Maybe I shouldn't ask," I said. Billy continued to pour a white powder into the bucket and stirred the liquid with a paint stick. "I don't think the ball is dissolving," I said.

"Tri-sodium-phosphate," he said.

"I was worried you were going to say something about eye of newt," I offered. "Are we baptizing it?"

Billy ignored me. "TSP is a degreaser. It will get the oil out of my ball, and I'll get my hook back. Witness this carefully. It's truly a miracle."

Billy had been an excellent bowler his first few years in Lyle, but that was before he gained seventy-five pounds and added seven inches to his waist. According to Terry McAdams, the best bowler in Lyle, Billy's hook deserted him because he had to release the ball far to his right to avoid his gut. No one had ever had the courage to explain the problem to Billy in those terms, and I wasn't going to be the first.

"Look here. Look at the surface of the water."

I looked into the drywall bucket. "Okay. What am I looking at?"

"The oil! See the oil that's come to the top? My hook is going to come back. Praise God. I'm going to get five boards of break minimum. You'll understand how this works when you get better." (I had been bowling about four months and my average was three pins below Billy's.)

Apparently, Billy's prayers had not been answered. The ball left his hand with no discernible rotation and headed for the gutter with no chance of hooking back. He finally gave up and took a seat in the settee, staring at the floor. "I don't know what the Lord is trying to tell me," he said as I approached. "I can't imagine what I did to deserve this humiliation, nor can I see what to do to avoid it."

I took a chance. "Go with what the Lord is giving you," I said reverently. "A straight ball that can hit whatever you want it to."

Billy stared at me. "You're kidding? The best you can offer me is go with the flow?"

"Or bowl a zero," I replied, shrugging.

"You have a point," he said.

Sheriff Belamy took his ball from his bag, approached the lane, and crushed the pocket with a seven-board hook. I heard Billy groan, then watched as he lined up in the middle of the alley and rolled the ball toward the headpin. The pins scattered, leaving a wobbling five-pin. He hesitated at the foul line, then turned to me, a hopeful smile on his face.

I rolled a few practice balls, then found Sarah Mosby, Reilly

Heartwood's sister, and Doc at a table just behind the lanes. Sarah is a feisty seventy-year-old who intimidates everyone. She used to smoke unfiltered cigarettes and still likes to drink beer. When provoked, she can cuss like a farmhand, but what provokes her no one quite knows. As a child, a visit to her house was always stressful, made more so by warnings from Reilly and my mother to be careful not to break anything. I remember being so nervous that I was afraid to use the bathroom. I suspect Sarah cultivated this image because it got her what she wanted. But when it mattered, she was caring and almost likeable.

"Cali told me what happened to Sydney Vail and that chimp," said Sarah, "and how she figured out that Sydney's been framed. I don't understand why you let them take the chimp, but I guess you had your reasons."

I felt the sting of the last remark, but did my best to ignore it. "She told you that?" I asked.

Sarah nodded. "I'm glad she convinced you to do something about this Sydney Vail."

"Cali twisted my arm," I said agreeably.

"Men always need convincing," said Sarah.

Billy joined us, a large mug of beer in his hand.

"I need another beer," said Sarah. "Anyone want anything?"

I asked for a draft and offered to pay. Sarah, pointing to my wallet on the table, responded that I already was paying and disappeared into the crowd.

A voice boomed over the PA that league play would start in ten minutes. "You seem distracted," said Billy. "I mean, more than usual."

I took a deep breath and let it out slowly. "Sometimes I get to thinking that people aren't so bad, and then I get among them and they prove me wrong."

"We humans look better from a distance," agreed Billy. "Any particular quality of the human beast that has you burning your *Homo sapiens* membership card?"

I couldn't bring myself to talk specifically about Kikora or chimps or cages. Instead, I offered up a more general complaint. "I'm having trouble understanding why we are so cruel to animals. I guess it's inherent in our species. Why else would we have passed a thousand laws to make it a crime to do heinous things? Howard Doring says it's because we were made in the image of God and sit on top of the evolutionary scale. I don't get it."

Billy brought his hands together at the fingertips. "He's quoting Saint Thomas Aquinas. Are you familiar with the 'Great Chain of Being'?"

I shook my head.

"Like a lot of other ideas passed on to us by the great Greek philosophers, it was intended to describe the world of their day. According to the Great Chain, all life is arranged like a ladder. Simple creatures occupy the low rungs, man the top rung. The lower rung dwellers serve those residing on the higher rungs. Saint Thomas Aquinas adopted chain thinking. He wrote that the imperfect are for the use of the perfect—animals make use of plants, and humans make use of both plants and animals. Since man was made in the image of God, man is above animals and can do what he wants with and to them." Billy shook his head. "Historically, the Christian religion, for all its admirable qualities, has never been animal friendly."

The commencement of league play was heralded by a loud horn that made me jump from my chair. I took a sip of Billy's beer. "Well, there you have it," I said.

My average for the night was a tad above a hundred and ten. Billy broke two hundred in one game. I wouldn't have cared except my team lost by twenty pins.

It was midnight when I returned to the poor farm. The night was still and thick. The moon had set, leaving the sky a black, endless canopy decorated with the summer constellations. I sat on the edge of the porch, four empty beer cans at my feet, staring into the darkness with unseeing eyes, unsure what might be staring back with malevolent intentions. "Come and get me," I yelled. A preemptive strike is always a good strategy against monsters that can't be seen.

I considered that the first *Homo sapiens* had once looked into the darkness with the same uneasiness. I wondered if those first humans were as devious and hateful as their progeny.

Howard Doring had justified testing on animals by declaring that humans were made in the image of God. Were the people who had lied about me, who had betrayed me and sent me to prison, made in the image of God? Were the terrorists who flew planes into the World Trade Center and the Pentagon, killing thousands of innocent people, made in the image of God? Was Reilly's killer or Dr. Stone's killer made in the image of God? How about the sick person who coaxed a lovable old cat like Van Gogh to approach, then violently slashed off his ear? I thought of Van Gogh and how he had probably run happily to the human who called to him. I imagined how he swiped his attacker, a feline gesture that means "good to see you." I wondered what Van Gogh would say about humans, to humans, if he could speak. How do humans, knowing the cruelty we as a species are capable of, stake claim to such a relationship with the Supreme Being?

"Fuck!" I screamed. I listened, but heard nothing.

Fuck was right. Something was stalking me. It wasn't a beast of flesh and bones. My pursuer was a creation of my mind. In prison, the beast was known as "the empties"—a state of mind in which the future looks as bleak as the present, and where nothing is worth hoping for. A prisoner wrestling with the empties was dangerous and unpredictable. Many a hapless inmate escaped life by hanging himself or by cutting his wrists. A few inmates picked fights that couldn't be won.

Like other inmates, I thought the empties attacked the weak. I was right, only I underestimated the power of prison to suck the life from me and make me vulnerable. When I doubted that anyone remembered me, when I gave up hope of proving my innocence, when I learned of my mother's terminal illness, the empties were close by, waiting. On my release, even after being vindicated of the crimes that wrongly sent me to prison, I couldn't escape the empties. Friends spoke of "picking up the pieces," but why start over when what you acquire can be taken from you without cause? Having nothing is having nothing to lose. The empties were again whispering inside my head.

As I stared into the darkness, I felt the presence of the beast. Sydney would be convicted of a crime I believe she didn't commit. Kikora would die because she was helpless. Regardless of whom I talked to or what I did, I wasn't going to save them. Celia Stone, who had dedicated her life to her job, had died violently, alone, and with only a guilt-ridden sister to grieve for her. Such was life as seen through the empties.

I caught a glimpse of the headlights coming up the driveway, the beams carving a tunnel in the darkness. A car pulled up to the walkway and the headlights went out. A female form emerged from the grayness at the edge of my vision, the apparition materializing as if from thin air. I thought it was Cali, but as the beer fog in my head lifted, the form morphed into Heather. She sat next to me, wrapping her arms around her legs and propping her head on her knees. I could smell her hair and feel her warmth. She gazed at me through empathetic eyes.

"What are you doing here?" I asked.

"The way you sounded on the phone, I thought you might need

some company," she replied.

I had a vague recollection of talking to Heather but no memory of what I might have said. I wasn't sure I wanted to remember.

"Are you going to offer me a beer?" she asked.

"I'm sorry. It's not real cold," I said, retrieving the last can from the box.

"I'm the one who owes you an apology," she said, popping the tab. "Leaving you that tape was a stupid thing to do. When I'm passionate about something, I can sometimes be an in-your-face kind of person." She took a long drink from the can, stifled a burp, and then smiled at me. "Sometimes I have a hard time thinking that anything I do matters. I heard that in your voice when I called you. I guess I needed some company myself."

"Company is good," I said, feeling my gloom lifting.

Heather slipped off the porch and strolled onto the lawn. "You don't see stars like this in Bethesda," she said, gazing skyward.

"Light pollution," I offered. "I doubt many city folk have ever seen the Milky Way."

She extended her hand. "Join me."

I stood up. "If you're going to stargaze, you need pillows and blankets."

Properly equipped, we studied the late-night constellations—Lyra, Sagittarius, and Scorpius—until we fell asleep. Somewhere in the night, I awoke with Heather's head resting on my shoulder. The empties had departed, and life mattered again.

CHAPTER
SIXTEEN

Thursday morning I awoke on my front lawn coiled in a blanket. I vaguely recalled Heather rolling away from me sometime during the night, and hearing the sound of a car starting. Her visit, like my bout with the empties, seemed like a distant memory. And yet, somehow and in some undefined way, Heather had eased her way into my life. I thought about Heather, Cali, and Bradley for a few moments and tried to make sense of it until I just couldn't deal with the complexities. Solving those equations would have to wait for another time.

I showered, picked up a double espresso mocha from Java Java, then went to my office. The first order of business was to feed Van Gogh and check to see if he'd brought Robbie any more gifts of prey. I checked messages again, made a few notes, then took the videotape that Heather brought me and headed back to my car.

Charlottesville, and my appointment with Theo, was a ninety-minute drive away. I plugged in my cell phone and began calling my client list. Only one of my clients was actually angry with me, and even that client mellowed when it became clear the delay was due to his failure to send me long-promised documents.

Charlottesville is south and slightly west of Lyle but still on the eastern slope of the Blue Ridge Mountains. I found myself on back roads and in small towns made familiar by the many trips I'd taken as a child with my mother and Reilly, trips that were occasionally referred to as "missions." I learned that the difference between a trip and a mission was the destination. A "trip" would end up at a stream or picnic area, or maybe the house of a relative. A "mission" usually involved someone who was sick, facing some personal tragedy, or living in squalor or a nursing home that smelled of the dying. Mostly, I have fond memories of these excursions and relived them happily until I reached the four-lane highway that would take me to Charlottesville and my meeting with Theo Levitz.

We'd agreed to meet in front of Clark Hall on the grounds of the University of Virginia. Built in the 1930s, Clark Hall had been the home of the law school until the mid-seventies, when the school was relocated to more modern facilities a few miles away. Clark ultimately came to house the Science and Engineering Library. As an undergrad engineering student, I spent many hours in Clark Hall, and almost as many sitting on the wall outside the building watching the throngs of students shuttling between classes and the undergraduate dorms.

I graduated from law school nearly eight years ago, long enough to be considered an experienced lawyer and not so long ago to have forgotten my days as a student. I grew up here in Charlottesville. I learned to think here. And I met Anna, my ex-wife, here. I can still see her, her bright smile and golden hair setting her off from the crowd. I can even remember the day when she first looked at me. Cupid's arrow couldn't have been more on target. We were married the summer I graduated from law school.

Before I went to prison, Anna and I lived out our collective dream. We were two young professionals with well-paying jobs and the social opportunities that money buys. We were in love, or so I thought, until just before the end of my trial. As the testimony against me mounted, the jury stopped listening. Anna, I suspect, sensed the jury's verdict before I did. As my fate became obvious, she withdrew, her body language conveying anger. She held me responsible for bringing our fairytale life to an end. The day I was sentenced, she left the courtroom without a word. I haven't seen or heard from her since.

As I revisited those times, I was struck by how detached I'd become from my past, as if my memories were a movie of some other person's life. All that had happened to me before my trial was an illusion, a creation of my naiveté. My life actually began when I went to prison. That's where I learned about reality, about power, and about those who wield it.

I was sitting on the wall when I saw Theo Levitz coming toward me. Theo is short, has graying curly hair, and large eyeballs that seem to drift independently in their sockets. Despite his unconventional appearance, Theo, at age forty-five, has a national reputation as an expert on constitutional law. He stopped in front of me, hands on his hips, glaring. "You missed your calling," he said. "Don't expect me to forgive you."

"Ever?"

A crooked smile erupted on Theo's face. "In my will," he said, "I will offer you penance." He slapped me on the shoulder. "You look pretty good for an ex-con. Let's take a walk and you can tell me what you're up to. I understand you want to file a law suit, but not much more."

"The Lawn" of the University of Virginia looks much like Thomas Jefferson first envisioned it. Along a rolling rectangle of grass are rooms that serve as student housing. Jefferson once said his greatest accomplishments were the creation of the University, along with the drafting of the Declaration of Independence and the Virginia statute for religious freedom. We strolled up the brick sidewalk toward the Rotunda while I went through Kikora's story. I glanced occasionally at Theo's roving eyes for any hint as to his professional assessment of Kikora's case. He nodded a few times but gave no clue as to what he was thinking. Finally, he took a seat on the steps of the Rotunda. "I'm familiar with several treatises arguing for legal rights for primates. What's *your* argument?"

"The essence of my argument is that our legal institutions are based on the equal treatment of equals," I replied. "Equality is an inalienable right. If we recognize these rights in humans, then we are compelled to recognize these rights in non-humans who are similarly situated."

"Give me an example," commanded Theo in his practiced professorial tone.

"The law recognizes the legal rights of children. It also recognizes the legal rights of the mentally impaired. No one would argue that either of these classes of people is fully cognizant or completely rational, but no one except Howard Doring would suggest we should lock them in cages or perform scientific tests on them. Chimpanzees are as cognizant as these individuals and should therefore have the same rights under the constitutional principle of equality."

"I'm sure you have evidence to support your claim?"

"I have an expert witness who can provide all the scientific data you want," I replied. I handed him Heather's phone number. "Anyway, I would then argue that denial of rights for incarcerated chimpanzees violates the Thirteenth Amendment prohibiting slavery."

Theo patted the marble step, and I sat next to him. "Do you know what would happen if the U.S. recognized chimpanzees as humans? I suspect you don't, and neither do I. But if Kikora has rights, so do all chimps in this country. As a matter of foreign policy, we would have to recognize the rights of chimpanzees in the wild. The hunting and capturing of wild chimps could invoke treaties against genocide. And I haven't even touched the economic consequences. You're not just running uphill here. You're trying to fly."

I sat for a moment, trying to fashion a rational response.

Finding none, I exploded. "I don't give a shit about consequences," I said. "A century and half ago, the same argument was made on why blacks should remain enslaved. Sixty years ago, it was Jews and retarded people. The world survived the correction of its moral compass then, and it can survive an enlightened view of primates today."

"So you're passionate," said Theo.

"I'm also out of time," I responded. "The tests on Kikora and her cellmates begin in less than two weeks. We need to delay the tests or the chimps will die."

I saw the answer in Theo's face. "We can't be prepared to file such a case in that amount of time," he said. "We have to overcome a lot of procedural issues first, not the least of which is standing. I can file for a restraining order, but I doubt the court would even docket the action, at least not without a bond."

I rubbed my temples for a moment, then stood up. "You've defended the right of white Nazis to demonstrate," I said. "You've argued passionately on behalf of blacks, the disabled, and aliens seeking asylum." I opened my briefcase and removed the videotape I'd received from Heather. "Watch this," I said handing it to him, "then call me. I'll be home late tonight or tomorrow morning. But Theo, don't watch it after you eat."

CHAPTER
SEVENTEEN

S taunton is to the west of Charlottesville across the Blue Ridge Mountains. Cali and I had arranged to meet Henry Thomas at a coffee shop in Staunton, and Cali was there when I arrived.

Before the Revolutionary War, Augusta County, where Staunton is located, took in the territories that would become the states of Kentucky, Ohio, Indiana, and Illinois, most of West Virginia, and a portion of western Pennsylvania, including what is now Pittsburgh. Staunton was a trading center for those traveling west and later was a major supply hub for the armies of the Confederacy. President Woodrow Wilson was born in Staunton in the 1850s. I learned all of this from Reilly, who had accused me of not listening during our many trips and missions.

Cali and I caught one another up on our respective travels. I managed to give my report without mentioning Heather. After twenty minutes, the conversation took on a forced quality and we fell into a tedious silence. Cali stared into her coffee cup. "I know we've only been at this for two days," she said, "but I have to tell you I haven't found a trail that I think takes us anywhere. I've interviewed a half dozen people, and each of them had nasty things to say about Celia, but I don't see any of these folks as a suspect. I have another six or seven possibles on my list. We should talk to Henry..."

"If he shows," I said, interrupting.

"We should talk to Henry and to the other people that Celia

knew," continued Cali, "but the only way we're going to find Celia's killer, assuming it isn't Sydney, is to get lucky."

"Then we have to make our own luck," I said.

"And what if we don't get lucky before Celia goes to trial?" asked Cali. "How long do you intend to pursue this?"

I ignored her question. "Read me the names on your list," I said.

Cali retrieved a PDA from her purse. "Steven Cartwright, Celia's neighbor, threatened Celia in front of the police. Cartwright's dog was pooping in Celia's yard. Celia complained a few times, then fed the dog a laxative. The dog crapped all over Cartwright's house, then mysteriously died. A civil suit was pending when Stone died."

"You're kidding?" I said. "She killed the neighbor's dog?"

"It's hard to say, but the cops I talked to said—pardon the pun—she was *stone cold* about the whole thing. Anyway, another suspect is Alex Crabtree, the owner of a café in Byron's Corner. Apparently, Stone asked for decaf and got high-test. The waitress apologized and brought her decaf, but then Stone complained it was cold. Stone was so abusive that the waitress became nervous and dropped the coffee on the table. Stone refused to pay the bill and insisted the waitress be fired. Alex stepped in and agreed to forgive the bill, but Stone wasn't mollified. An argument ensued and Alex allegedly shoved Stone. In retaliation, Stone pepper sprayed Alex and left."

"Nice lady," I said.

"She wasn't done yet," responded Cali. "Health inspectors showed up the next day and cited the café for a dozen violations. Alex couldn't afford the fine or the improvements and had to close the restaurant. From the pepper spray, he also suffered some loss of vision in his right eye and was suing Stone for damages."

"It's obvious she was lacking in basic social skills," I said.

"I have more if you're interested."

I was spared a response by the appearance of a young sour-faced man who was both overweight and, by first impressions, over-bearing. "Are you the insurance adjusters?"

Cali nodded. "That we are. And you must be Henry Thomas."

"I don't have a lot of time," he said.

"Won't take long," I said, "but it would better if you sat down."

Henry plopped himself into a chair and looked at his watch.

"I'm sure you heard what happened to Celia Stone," offered Cali. "We need to understand what you remember about her. It's just routine."

Henry folded his arms across his chest and rested them on his protruding belly. "I remember she fired me because she said I left a bottle of re-agent on a lab table," he said. "I denied it, and she canned me. That's the way she was. She didn't take backtalk from anyone, even the big dogs. I'm not surprised someone slapped her around."

"Sounds like you would have enjoyed doing it yourself," said Cali.

The implications of the question weren't lost on Henry. "I said a few things I didn't mean," he said, "but I left town instead. Are we done?"

"You can prove that?" pressed Cali.

"Yeah, I can prove it," snapped Henry.

"Can I get you anything?" I asked. "Coffee, a sandwich?"

"I'm good," he said, "and I've got to get back to the office."

"Just one more thing," I said. "You mentioned that Celia didn't take lip from the big dogs. What did you mean?"

"I heard Celia and Arthur Collins, the head of security at DMI, shouting at each other on a couple of occasions, you know, the nights I worked late. Arthur didn't like her much, but Celia was a favorite of Howard Doring, the chairman of the board, so Arthur couldn't do much about it."

"What were they arguing about?" asked Cali.

"Arthur wanted Celia to start testing the diet drug in June," answered Henry. "Celia said the chimpanzees weren't healthy enough to start the tests then." Henry shrugged. "Right after the argument, Celia called Mr. Doring and Arthur backed off, but the whole thing made Celia pissy. I guess that's why she fired me." He stood up. "That's all I know. I've got to go."

"Well, that was a dead-end," said Cali after Thomas was out of earshot.

I nodded in apparent agreement, but a voice inside my head replied, "Not quite."

Cali and I drove in separate cars to Harvey's office in Byron's Corner. I hadn't spoken with Harvey since the hearing at the poor farm, which seemed like eons ago, but which, in reality, was just two days ago. The clock seemed to be moving fast—two days gone on Judge McKenna's 14-day moratorium, during which DMI could not test its new anti-obesity drug on Kikora or the other DMI chimps.

When we stepped inside, Harvey was sitting at his computer. He looked at us, the expression on his face an odd mix of surprise and panic. It was then I noticed the pint bottle of whiskey on his desk. The bottle was lying on its side, the top of it pointed at Harvey.

"Hey Harv," I said softly. "How are you?"

His eyes danced from me to Cali. "Not so good," he said, licking his lips.

"I can see that," I replied, taking a seat in front of his desk. "Looks like your demons have been talking to you."

His expression softened. "You know about them?"

"Oh yeah. I know about them."

Cali moved behind me, her hands touching my shoulders. "You can't listen to them," offered Cali. "They lie."

Harvey nodded. "I spoke with Sydney last night," replied Harvey, his eyes fixed on the bottle. "She didn't kill Celia Stone. I believe her. But she doesn't want to live her life in prison. She asked me to help her die. She begged me to bring her some pills." He closed his eyes and pressed his lips together. "She knows I can't help her, either as a lawyer or as her appointed angel of death."

A shiver ran through me. Harvey and I were in the same place, fighting futility and blaming ourselves. I'd wanted to run away. Harvey wanted to hide inside a bottle. "You can't help her drunk," I said.

I handed Harvey the permission letter I'd received from Melissa. "Cali and I were going to the scene of the crime to look around. Want to come?"

"Shep will take us to lunch when we're done," said Cali.

Harvey took a deep breath, then slipped the bottle into the bottom drawer of his desk. "Thanks," was all he could muster.

I called Detective Reggie Mason from Harvey's office, then drove Cali, Harvey, and myself to Celia Stone's house. When we arrived, Reggie was waiting for us. "I'm not sure why you're here," he said to me, then looked at Cali. "I'm guessing you're Ms. McBride. I saw you at the farm the other day but didn't have a chance to introduce myself. You wrote the articles about Reilly Heartwood. I really enjoyed them."

"Thanks," she said. "The name's Cali."

I showed Reggie the letter from Melissa. "Looks official," he said, barely reading the document.

"Has Stone's house been cleared of evidence?" I asked.

"Yeah," said Reggie.

I persisted. "We're here to look around."

The others looked at each other. "Not much to see," replied

Reggie. "I've been over it a dozen times myself, but you can take a look if you want."

He handed each of us a pair of gloves, a shower cap, and shoe covers. "The house has been released, but if you come up with another suspect, I'd like to be able to claim that the crime scene wasn't corrupted. Don't touch anything unless you're wearing gloves."

Reggie retrieved a folder from his car, then led us to the front of the house. He slipped under the crime scene tape, took a key from the folder, and unlocked the front door. Cali, Harvey, and I followed and joined him in a small foyer. The air inside was warm, stale, and slightly pungent.

"You might want to turn on the AC," I said, fanning myself.

"We didn't want to stir up any hairs or fibers," he replied. He disappeared for a moment, then returned as the AC fan motor kicked in. "I don't think it matters that much," he said, obviously discouraged.

To the left of the foyer was a small dining room, maybe ten-foot square. To its right was a slightly larger living room. The carpet bore a dark stain inside a chalked border. "That's where she died," said Reggie.

Cali and I entered the room slowly, almost reverently. I'm not certain what a scientist earns, but Celia Stone was either poor or liked to live that way. The furniture was probably cheap looking even when it was new. Looking at the couch, I could see that one of the cushions sank nearly to the floor. I got down on my knees and looked under a lamp table, then noted that the back of the couch was arched so its back legs didn't touch the wall.

"What are you doing?" asked Cali.

"Pretending to be a frightened chimpanzee," I replied as I got to my feet.

Cali's face softened as the implications became clear. "Kikora?"

"Maybe," I said with a shrug. "There's a blanket back there. In the bunkhouse at the farm, Kikora made a nest from old blankets."

We wandered through Dr. Stone's house like tourists. Viewing what remains of a life is intrusive and irreverent. Had she known that her time on earth was about to expire, she might have left her world a little differently, choosing the things that her post-death visitors would see and would not see, creating her own last impression. As it was, Stone's house was as she lived in it.

After twenty minutes, I realized that something was missing. "Did you notice that our dead doctor is big on clutter?" I asked Cali as we stepped out of an upstairs bedroom.

"Your point?" asked Cali.

"My point is that she wasn't obsessed with order, and she wasn't one to leave a space unfilled."

"What difference does that make?" asked Harvey.

I looked at Reggie. "You told me earlier that the crime scene had been scrubbed, yet you were able to find traces of blood and a few fingerprints."

"That's right," said Reggie. "What're you driving at?"

I led them back to the bathroom off the master bedroom. "Open the medicine cabinet and tell me what you see."

Cali complied and the door swung open, revealing three neatly arranged shelves of over-the-counter products and medications. "The woman was over fifty," I said, "and she hasn't any prescription drugs. Nothing for pain, menopause, or insomnia—even a leftover antibiotic. Maybe some people are lucky enough to avoid going to the doctor, but most of us have some evidence of being sick."

"She's not that healthy," said Cali, "and we know that she's not that neat."

"I'm still not sure what the point is," said Reggie.

"It looks to me like someone took her prescription drugs," I said. "The question is which ones and why." I stared into the cabinet, then looked at Reggie. "Was she on anything?"

"The toxicology results show traces of Zoloft," he answered, "but a lot of people take Zoloft. I don't see that taking us anywhere."

"Then where is it?" I asked, pressing the point.

"If someone took it, they must have had a reason," offered Harvey.

"You've got that look," said Cali to me, a touch of hope in her voice. "Let's hear it."

"You won't like it, and I can't support it," I replied.

"Sounds like a conversation best had over lunch," said Harvey, his demeanor much like the day we first met.

"I don't think you should talk in front of me anyway," said Reggie.

We filed out of the bathroom and regrouped in the driveway. "Thanks, Reggie," I said. "That was very helpful."

He looked at me. "Don't go playing lawyer on me," he said. "I'm looking for the truth, not trying to help you find a crack in the law to spring Sydney Vail."

"Reggie, do I sense your trust in me waning?"

"You can't help looking for legal loopholes any more than a polecat can stop smelling like one," replied Reggie. "I just want to be sure we're on the same side." He studied me for a moment. "Geez. Never mind."

"Join us for lunch," I said, "and I will restore your confidence."

He nodded reluctantly. "Just remember, the Miranda warning will be in effect there," he said.

Harvey directed us to a restaurant five miles outside of town. "You will not believe the way they cook fish. Broiled, poached, fried, grilled, and blackened—any way they prepare it, it's amazing. And they've got the best hushpuppies in the county and the best fruit pies in the Commonwealth." Talk of food seemed to buoy his spirits.

As seemed to be the custom, we ate first, then talked over coffee. My theory wasn't fully developed, and it wouldn't have bothered me in the least if the subject had never come up. But Cali wasn't going to let that happen.

"I'm full," she said, "and now I'm ready to hear what Shep learned from our trip to Celia Stone's house that the rest of us mere mortals missed."

"I'd prefer to wait," I replied, "until the idea is at least half-baked."

"Sydney and I are going to trial in a few weeks," said Harvey. "I've got devils telling me there's no hope. All things considered, I wouldn't mind hearing any theory as long as it doesn't involve aliens and Agent Mulder."

"Okay," I answered reluctantly. "Let's start with Sydney's story. She says she visited Celia in the morning, was scratched by both Celia and Kikora in a scuffle, and left without the chimp. When she came back at five, Celia was dead. Sydney knew that Kikora liked to hide behind the couch and found her easily. Kikora was sedated by this time and didn't put up a fight. Accepting that as true, the killer must have arrived after Sydney's morning visit, killed Celia, and left. After Sydney took the chimp, the killer must have returned to clean up the scene. Otherwise we would have found Sydney's fingerprints."

I saw doubt creep into the faces of Reggie, Cali, and Harvey. "The killer didn't notice the chimp?" asked Harvey.

"I understand your hesitation, but Celia would have told her killer that the chimp was already gone," I replied. "Why would the killer doubt her? Kikora's cage is empty and her nest behind the couch is pretty well hidden unless you get down on the floor."

"But then what's the motive for the murder?" asked Cali.

I nodded. "Yeah. Exactly. We are currently chasing two possible motives—either someone killed Celia to get the chimp, or someone killed Celia because they had a grudge against her. If we eliminate Sydney, it appears that the chimp wasn't the reason for the killing. That seems to lead us to a more standard motive—jealousy, revenge, or robbery. Cali's list of grudge-bearers looks like the local census, so that seems like the right place to start."

"You keep qualifying everything," said Harvey. "Exactly what are you saying?"

"He's saying," said Reggie, "that the average person wouldn't have taken the time to wipe the house for fingerprints and wouldn't have a reason to steal Celia's medication and selectively delete files from her computer."

"I think there's a third motive," I continued. "It is possible that she was killed *because* she was going to give the chimp away."

Cali looked at me in disbelief. "You're not suggesting that someone at DMI killed Celia Stone?"

"I'm only saying that we need to consider it as a possibility," I said. "Given the amount of time we have left, we need to focus our energies where they will do the most good. We need a suspect with the motive and means to explain all the loose ends in this case. My instincts tell me that we are dealing with a killer who was threatened in some way by what Celia knew or had written on her computer. The killer is a professional criminal who knows enough about crime scenes to eliminate a lot of the evidence. I'm not sure why the medication was stolen, but just the fact that someone went to that much trouble reinforces my belief that it isn't a neighbor whose dog was killed with a laxative."

"What do you think, Reggie?" asked Harvey.

Reggie pursed his lips. "I agree with the profile. I'm not sure I understand why DMI would want to kill its chief scientist."

"Well?" asked Harvey. "What about that?"

All eyes were on me. "Henry Thomas said that Celia had an

argument with Arthur Collins, the head of security at DMI, about the progress of the test program involving the chimpanzees. If DMI had learned that Celia was going to give up Kikora, I can imagine a confrontation between Collins and Celia. DMI would certainly have a reason to hide Celia's mutiny from the stockholders. Perhaps they would want to hide her emotional condition as well, and that's why the prescriptions are missing. But I'm just speculating. My point is we can't ignore Collins or any other suspect just because he or she works for DMI."

As the silence grew, I leaned back in my chair and sipped my coffee. "I'm not drawing a conclusion," I said. "I'm saying we need to open another branch of our investigation. We still need to look at Celia's life and sort through the normal list of suspects."

"Investigating DMI isn't going to be easy in this town," said Harvey, obviously disappointed.

I sensed the group's growing opposition to this line of argument, and decided to redirect the conversation. "We need to put our resources where they will do the most good," I said. "The first thing we need to do is find the doctor who prescribed the Zoloft. Maybe the doctor will be able to testify that Stone was going to give the chimp to Sydney."

"I like that part," said Harvey, "because, as things now stand, the prosecution is saying Sydney went to Stone's house to murder Stone and steal the chimp. But if we demonstrate that Sydney didn't have felonious intent, then we have a good chance of getting the murder one charge reduced."

"And?" asked Cali.

"If we can reduce the charge," I replied, "she'd be facing ten to twenty years instead of life. Of course, she'd still be in jail."

"It's progress," said Harvey, sounding as if he were trying to convince himself.

I turned to Reggie. "Of all the suspects we have listed, the only one with a serious criminal record is Devon Sheen. It would be helpful if I knew where he was and what he was up to."

"I hear you," said Reggie.

"That's it?" pressed Cali. "That's your agenda?"

"That's it," I replied.

Cali gave me a skeptical look, but said nothing more.

"Well, then," said Harvey, "I think we've made progress."

I finished my coffee while the others chatted. The importance of chasing down Devon Sheen and the doctor who prescribed Celia's Zoloft wasn't lost on me, but neither was I certain that either of those leads would answer the question that consumed me 24/7: Who killed Celia Stone? Logic pointed toward Sydney Vail as the prime candidate. But logic couldn't adequately explain Reggie's loose ends. My instinct was compelling me to look at DMI for that explanation, and at Arthur Collins and Jonathan Freeman in particular. Jonathan Freeman had told Harvey that Arthur Collins set him up. I wasn't sure what that meant, but I was determined to find out.

As I sipped my coffee, I was also keenly aware that my suspicions about DMI were not completely rational. I had disliked Howard Doring from the moment I read about his attitude toward biomedical testing, animal rights, and the dominance of human kind. Howard Doring epitomized all of humanity's worst qualities without any of its redeeming ones. That Kikora's fate was in his hands was galling. I wanted to hurt Howard Doring, to deny him the satisfaction of his chain thinking, to bring him down.

The challenge for me was to stay objective and to be patient. Glancing at Cali, doubt and worry evident in her eyes, I realized I was neither.

CHAPTER
EIGHTEEN

Friday was a day of waiting. Gus was working on locating Jonathan Freeman. Reggie was trying to track down Devon Sheen without getting into trouble with his superiors. Cali was catching up on sleep and working on her story. And Theo Levitz would only say he had been in contact with Heather and was considering various options regarding legal action to protect Kikora. I found his reference to Heather annoying because I hadn't been able to reach her by phone despite repeated attempts.

I searched for something I could do to advance Sydney's cause. I tried to log-in to Celia Stone's e-mail address but quickly grew weary of typing in random passwords. I went through the forgotten-password procedure, only to be confronted by a mnemonic in the form of a question: "What is your pet's name?" According to Melissa, Celia didn't have any pets. I tried Kikora, Fluffy, Rover, Spike, and Kitty before giving up.

On Friday morning, I visited a client in McLean, a few miles from D.C. Afterward, I took a trip to the zoo, but Jerome wasn't there. I left several messages for Heather, but didn't receive a return call until just before six. "Hello, Shep. This is Heather."

"Hello," I said, pulling my Honda to the side of the road. "You left so early the other morning I didn't have time to talk or to ask you to dinner."

My invitation was met with an uneasy silence. Finally, she said,

"I'm involved in a situation. I think you are too. Maybe when these things are clarified, I might enjoy dinner and stars and warm beer. But I don't want to go down that path the way things are right now."

My "situation" was Cali. Between Bradley's proposal and Heather's reluctance to see me again, I was being forced to deal with my "situation" and resolve it. Deciding on Heather excluded Cali. Conversely, deciding on Cali excluded Heather. I suspected Cali was facing the same issue in choosing between Bradley and me. The idea of a commune ran through my head, but didn't stick.

Heather spoke before I could formulate a response. "Why don't we talk later? I really have to go." She hung up.

I sat stunned for a moment, my thoughts swirling. Heather had unavoidably complicated my life, but with Sydney's life at stake, I didn't have time to uncomplicate it. With a deep breath, I pushed both Cali and Heather from my mind and pulled back onto the highway.

I stopped by the Bent Note, but the group performing wasn't keen on jamming with an amateur trumpet player. Even Gus was too busy for dinner. With no visible progress in Sydney's case and nothing else to do, I drank a beer while the band played some dragging off-key tune. I was back in Lyle by nine. Time, it seemed, was the enemy, and I was losing the war on all fronts.

The residents insisted on helping me find the shrink who had prescribed Zoloft to Celia Stone. I was well aware that she might have gotten the medication without a prescription—as samples or from a friend—but there was nothing to lose by trying, so I put the residents to work searching the Web for pharmacies near Byron's Corner. Using the Internet yellow pages, they started searching within ten miles of town, increasing the radius in ten-mile increments. The residents pretended to be calling from a doctor's office in Florida on behalf of a patient who claimed she needed a refill of her Zoloft prescription. The

Florida doctor needed to talk with the prescribing doctor before writing the replacement prescription. Naturally, the patient was crazy and couldn't remember who the doctor was. The pharmacists quickly related to the image of a crazy vacationer off her meds and willingly engaged in small talk about their latest experiences with whackos of both sexes. The residents took to the ruse quickly and, with their number blocked by Caller ID, were very convincing.

By Saturday morning, they had called all the listed pharmacies within forty miles. As the afternoon wore on, the search was extended to a hundred miles. I was on the phone with a client when my cell phone rang and Carrie announced that she'd found the doctor. She said something about celebrating their success and that I should come home.

When I arrived at Heartwood House, I called out but no one answered. I went to the kitchen but found no one there either. Then I heard voices coming from the patio and went outside. The residents, along with Cali and Frieda, were seated at a table drinking lemonade and chatting victoriously. A half dozen felines were chowing down on bowls of milk and leftover chicken, a clear indication that Frieda was in a party mood.

I took a seat, was immediately joined by Molly, a little black and white cat who jumped into my lap, spent a few minutes kneading my belly (what Reilly once described as "making bread dough"), then curled up in a ball and purred while I scratched her behind her ears. "The winning call was made by Harry," said Carrie. "He won a new computer, which we thought you'd pay for."

Cali smiled. "The prize was my idea," she said.

"I'm going to get a laptop," said Harry, "with a DVD player."

"Fine," I said, "but will someone please tell me who Celia's doctor actually is?"

"His name," answered Harry, "is Dr. Frank Lipton. He lives in Fairmount. The pharmacy there gave me his number. I wrote it all down just like you said."

"What's our next assignment?" asked Carrie.

I squeezed her hand. "Find me a map."

"I'll get it," said Frieda.

"You all did a great job," I said.

"Are you going to be able to save Kikora?" asked Cecil.

I shook my head. "I don't know, but I haven't given up hope."

My cell phone rang. "Shep, it's Gus. Mel told me that Jonathan Freeman is in hiding because two street contracts have been placed on him by sources unknown. I'm working on a couple of leads and will get back to you as soon I hear something."

"Thanks," I said. "Let's get to Freeman before he starts a worm farm."

Frieda arrived with a map and we located Fairmount on the rail line that runs along the eastern slope of the Appalachian Mountains, about a hundred miles north of Byron's Corner.

"Looks like more driving," said Cali.

I shook my head. "It's too late to go anywhere today. We can get an early start in the morning."

Cali and I settled into a weary silence, broken only by Molly's contented purrs. "You're thinking about something," said Cali. "Do you want to share?"

I scratched Molly, and she rolled on her back, exposing her tummy. "I'm thinking about a lot of things," I replied.

"I'm talking about the thing that's bugging you the most."

I nodded. "Yeah. Well it's the power thing. DMI had the power to get a prosecutor to indict Jonathan Freeman for murder without regard to the evidence. DMI had the power to negotiate his release. With that kind of leverage, the truth doesn't matter much."

"The truth always matters," replied Cali. "I believe you told me that."

I forced a smile. "Then it must be true," I said.

"All we have to do," she added, "is discover it."

I nodded in agreement. "The sooner the better."

CHAPTER
NINETEEN

Downtown Fairmount turned out to be little more than a traffic light, a train depot, and a couple of blocks of small stores. The main drag was busy with Sunday shoppers, the traffic slowed by waves and shouts from passing friends.

Dr. Lipton lived and worked a few blocks from the main street in a large white frame house set in the middle of a half-acre lot. I parked in front, under the shade of a large oak, and as Cali and I stepped out of the car, I seemed to step back in time. Instead of the drone of air conditioners, I heard birds and insects and the distant squeal of children playing. Despite the heat, the windows of Dr. Lipton's house were open. Screens kept the bugs at bay.

Cali and I followed a flagstone walkway to a small porch, and I knocked on the screen door. The response came from behind us.

"May I help you?"

I turned and saw an elderly man in a straw hat and coveralls. He was holding a large clump of chickweed.

"I was looking for Dr. Lipton," I said.

"Your search is over, son, but I don't see patients any more." He studied me for a moment. "But neither of you look like patients. You're not selling anything, I hope, because you'd be wasting your time."

"No, sir," I said.

He nodded. "To non-patients, the name is Frank," he said.

"My name is Shep Harrington," I replied.

"My name is Cali."

Frank gave us a social nod. "I like to talk sittin' down," he said. "It's an old habit that's well-suited for an old body. Let's go around back and you can tell me why you two have come to the end of the earth to talk to an old man."

We followed Frank. I noted that he had a slight limp, probably from a bad hip. "It's been a hot summer, but the marigolds seem to like it," he said, gesturing toward a flowerbed on the side of the house. As we turned the corner, the landscape became a palette of colors. I stepped up on a brick patio and looked out at dozens of beds filled with flowers of all hues. Butterflies floated above what I thought were zinnias, and hummingbirds hovered and darted among bright red trumpet vines.

"Oh, my," I said, trying to take it all in.

"They're lovely," said Cali.

"Thank you," said Frank. "Sit down and I'll get us something to drink."

Frank returned with a pitcher of lemonade. "I don't like it too sweet," he said. "It may make you pucker," he said, handing me a glass, "but it'll kill a thirst."

I took a drink of lemonade. Frank was not exaggerating his aversion to sugar. Cali made a sour face. "It's certainly thirst quenching," she said.

Frank seemed to ignore us. "I take to flowers easily," he said, "but I'm not doing well with my tomatoes."

"Tomatoes like a low pH," I said. "Sometimes the things you put on your flowers can raise the pH to a level that keeps the roots from absorbing the nutrients. You'll get a big plant and no fruit."

He glanced at me with doubt written on his face. "Now, how does a young man like you come to know something about tomatoes?"

I laughed. "In prison, the warden assigned me the job of working his vegetable garden. The soil was full of construction waste and my first plants lasted about a week. He bought me a few garden books, and I watched all the garden shows on TV."

"Prison," he said solemnly. "I can't imagine what it's like being locked up." He shook his glass, swirling the ice and staring into space. Conversations, I gathered, were something he engaged in deliberately, like gardening. Finally, he said, "I seem to have forgotten to ask you why you're here."

I fell in step with his conversational cadence and let a moment pass. "We are looking into the death of Celia Stone," I said. "Some of the facts don't add up, and we were hoping you could fill in a few pieces of the puzzle."

"Celia was a patient," answered Frank. "You know that or you wouldn't be here. You also know that I can't talk about my patients."

"Ordinarily, I would agree with you," I replied. "But Celia was recently murdered, and an innocent person has been charged with the crime. As the accused's attorney, I believe she will be convicted if we don't get to the truth about what happened."

Frank regarded me with practiced but sincere compassion, a skill than none of my many therapists had acquired.

"And what is it that you expect me to do?"

"The person who killed Dr. Stone removed all of her prescription medicines, including the Zoloft you prescribed. I believe the killer knew she was seeing a therapist and didn't want anyone to know. I'm trying to understand why."

Frank closed his eyes and pressed his glass to his face. "That is indeed an interesting question. I really haven't a clue."

"Why do you think Celia Stone came to you?" I asked.

For a moment, I wasn't sure if he was going to answer. Then he said, "In the early sixties, I was involved in the debate over the source of language. The prevailing view, which I adamantly defended, was that through evolution, humans had acquired a brain function specifically for language acquisition. Of course, there was no proof of this brain appendage, but that didn't stop us from asserting its existence. The language lobe explained how we learned speech and why other animals would never be able to do so." Frank closed his eyes and shook his head. He emitted an audible groan. "What fools we were."

I struggled with impatience, but lost. "What does that have to do with…?" Frank waved his hand at me, and I swallowed my words.

"Arrogance," he said with a friendly laugh, "is not reserved to lawyers. The linguistic crowd operated under the unspoken principle that language totally separated us from the animal world. We were superior because we communicated. The gift of speech was from God. But reports about the sign language skills of a chimp named Washoe refuted our theory. Even so, a number of us fought the data. Unknowingly, or through arrogant indifference, we allowed the testing labs to abuse these creatures, and to use our theory as their justification. After all, animals had no concept of time, no free will, no sense of their situation." Frank looked away, then continued.

"I went to a test facility in Arizona, where the chimps were confined in small cages. I saw these poor creatures in a cell, struggling with isolation and madness. It occurred to me that if chimps could formulate sentences, they could think, feel, and have emotions. I remember crying in front of a cage, pleading with a female chimpanzee to forgive me." Frank swatted at an insect. "After that, I assisted with chimp studies until I retired from field work about ten years ago. I was a traitor in the eyes of people like Howard Doring. I think Celia Stone had arrived at an ethical crossroads regarding the use of chimpanzees as biomedical test subjects. I think that's why she sought me out."

"So you advised Dr. Stone on the morality of testing on chimpanzees." I had made a statement, not asked a question.

Frank regarded me with frustration. "You ask but you don't listen. She came to me because of my experience. She wanted to understand why I had changed my mind, not what I thought about her testing on chimps. She had no qualms about testing, at least none she shared with me." He shook his head. "Celia thought if she could just resolve her issues about a chimp she was caring for, her life would go back to the way it was. I tried to explain to her that she had serious emotional problems that needed a prescription and our collective attention. I recommended that she take time off from work to rest and to deal with a lifetime of issues, but she wouldn't hear of it. That would have ended her career, she said."

"Did she say anything about what she intended to do with the chimp?" I asked, still uncertain what Dr. Lipton was saying.

"Yes. Celia said she'd been approached by a woman about a chimp…"

"Kikora?" I interrupted.

"Yes," said Frank, "Kikora. Celia had apparently made up her mind to give the chimp to this woman, but she didn't say why or when. As I indicated, she wasn't rational or focused. In Celia's mind, all of her problems—her depression, her paranoia, her feelings of loneliness and despair—stemmed from her relationship with Kikora. Giving the chimp away and getting her out of the lab was her solution." Frank shrugged. "I suppose she was looking to me for reassurance that once the chimp was gone, she'd be better, but of course that's not what I told her."

"Did she mention Jonathan Freeman?" asked Cali.

Frank shook his head. "No. She only talked about this woman."

Another silence ensued, but I didn't care. Frank Lipton had just saved Sydney from a first-degree murder charge. I stood up, as did Cali. "Thank you, Dr. Lipton. You've been very helpful."

"Sit down," commanded Frank wearily. "I haven't told you everything yet."

We complied, and waited while Frank wrestled with his thoughts. "Celia told me she thought someone was following her, but she was unwilling or unable to say who that someone was, or what reason anyone would have to follow her. Such fears are also a symptom of depression, and so I wasn't alarmed by her claim. But a week or so after our first appointment, I began to notice things about my office. One day, a file drawer I'd closed was slightly open. Another day, I found the copy machine warm when I hadn't used it in days. Just after Celia died, I noticed her file was missing. Even then, I didn't make a connection to Celia's stalker. I thought I was just losing more of my memory.

"But then I received a call. The man didn't identify himself, and I didn't ask how he knew that Celia Stone was my patient, but he very politely explained that reporters were digging into the backgrounds of employees at Doring Medical and that he'd appreciate my respecting the privacy of Celia and the company by not talking to anyone. I was offered a tidy sum if I'd promise in writing not to disclose what I knew, but I told him to keep his money, that I wouldn't discuss such things anyway. To be honest, there was nothing in my file about the company. I only saw Celia three or four times, so my notes weren't that extensive either, other than to suggest that more treatment was advisable. Anyway, when you walked up, I thought you two might be from Doring Medical."

Cali and I thanked Dr. Lipton again, then headed back to the car.

"Well, that certainly muddied the waters," said Cali.

"Oh?" I said. "I thought what Frank told us made everything as clear as glass."

"Meaning what?" demanded Cali.

"DMI was on to Celia," I said confidently.

Cali grabbed my arm. "Then you heard what you wanted to hear. I know you believe someone from DMI is involved in this case, and you may be right. But we aren't any closer to knowing who killed Celia Stone than we were when we left Lyle this morning."

"What about the missing medical file?" I asked. "Frank said he found it missing *after* Celia died."

"What about it?" replied Cali. "Frank doesn't have a good handle on time. Did it occur to you that Celia might have had second thoughts about confiding in an old man and could have taken the file herself? Frank probably discovered it missing after he heard she'd been murdered."

Cali's explanation was annoyingly plausible, which, I supposed, proved Cali was right about my selective listening. "At least we have a witness who will testify that Sydney didn't go to Stone's house to commit murder," I said.

"We do, and that's great," replied Cali. "But you need to stay objective."

I nodded, but I wasn't concerned about my lack of objectivity. I was thinking about getting inside the DMI corporate psyche. To do that, I needed to find Jonathan Freeman alive and talk to him.

The trip back to Lyle seemed to take forever. I spoke several times with Harvey by cell phone about the implications of Dr. Lipton's disclosures. He was relieved, even ecstatic, to hear that we had a witness who would refute the prosecution's position that Sydney went to Stone's house with the intent to commit murder. Other than that, Harvey and I didn't agree on much. Cali, who eavesdropped on my half of the conversations, sided with Harvey.

"You can't prove that anyone at DMI knew before the murder that Stone was going to give up Kikora," insisted Harvey. "And you can't prove that someone from DMI removed the Zoloft prescription from Celia's medicine cabinet either. It isn't uncommon for companies to try and find out what someone may say if contacted by the press."

"Come on Harvey, that's why we need to go on a discovery blitz," I replied. "It's time to be aggressive. Let's find out what DMI knew and when they knew it. Draft subpoenas and discovery motions. Let's fire a shot over their bow. Let's tell them we're on to them, and then see what they do."

"We shoot over the bow," said Harvey, "and we may be hoisting ourselves on our own petard, if you'll forgive two clichés in one sentence. I'm not against being aggressive, but I am against taking needless chances with my client's life. Unless we can prove that DMI has evidence material to Sydney's defense, no judge in this county is going to grant us leave to go fishing in DMI's files or to compel their employees to talk to us. You just brought me the one piece of evidence I can use with the prosecutor to negotiate a reduction of the charges against Sydney. I'm not willing to fritter that chance away unless you have something better than what you've told me so far."

I didn't respond immediately. "You're her counsel," I said.

"Good of you to remember," said Harvey, who hung up.

I set my cell phone in the charger stand and focused on getting home without a speeding ticket. Cali, quiet for a half hour or so, finally chimed in. "You really believe that DMI is involved in Stone's murder."

I shrugged, and tried to sound objective. "I'm just saying it's a path we should explore."

Cali wasn't buying. "No, what you really mean is that your sixth sense is agitating you big time."

"Yeah, I can feel it," I admitted. "I can't explain it, but I can feel it. Harvey and you think I'm jamming the pieces of the puzzle together. I think any other explanation leaves too many of these pieces unexplained."

Cali didn't respond, returning instead to her silent mode. Another half-hour passed. The weather had gotten nasty. Wind-swept rain was drumming on the car, cutting visibility to a few car lengths. When my cell phone rang, Cali grabbed it.

"Hey Reggie," said Cali. She listened, nodding, but not speaking.

"What is he saying?" I demanded.

"You've located Devon Sheen," repeated Cali for my benefit. "Okay. Phone records show that Devon made two calls to Celia a week before she was murdered, and she called him once…Shep is listening…Yes. Hang on."

I gave her a quick glance and saw annoyance in her face. "What?"

"He doesn't want to give us Devon's address because he's afraid you might do something stupid," she said. "Which of course, given your track record, is a legitimate concern."

"Let me speak to him," I said.

Cali shook her head. "Only if you pull over."

I came to an overpass and pulled onto the shoulder. Then she handed me the phone. "What's the problem?" I said to Reggie.

"The problem is that there's a record of my request for Devon's phone records. You go showing up at his house making like Dirty Harry and someone's going to be asking questions about why I was checking up on him in the first place."

"I'll take him flowers and talk nice to him," I said, not hiding my frustration. "He's our best suspect. Someone's got to talk to him."

Reggie went silent for a moment. "Promise me you won't take

a weapon," he said.

"Scout's honor," I said.

"Write this down," he said.

Reggie gave me an address in Winchester and hung up.

Cali looked at me. "So?"

"We have an address for Devon," I said.

"Well, that's good news," said Cali. "At least, *I* think it's good news."

It was, in fact, great news. Even I couldn't deny that the phone records elevated Devon to suspect number one. He had a motive. He was a convicted professional criminal. As someone familiar with crime scene procedures, he might have been smart enough to destroy evidence before leaving. I was even ready to believe that he came back to clean the scene a second time. At least, I wanted to believe.

And yet, something was still bothering me. I was missing something, something obvious, something hiding in plain view. *Why couldn't I see it?* Maybe Devon would provide the missing piece of the puzzle. For Sydney's sake, and my peace of mind, I certainly hoped so.

CHAPTER
TWENTY

H aving Devon's address gave us choices, not answers. Cali and I spent the next few hours trying to decide how to approach Devon about Celia Stone. I suggested that one option was to go to his house, put a gun in his mouth, and ask him why had he killed Celia, but Cali wasn't keen on the idea, reminding me of my promise to Reggie. My other suggestion—that we tie him up, weight him down with rocks, and toss him in the Shenandoah River—was also not greeted with enthusiasm. "If he sinks, he's innocent," I suggested.

Cali's idea that she approach Devon as a reporter doing a story about con artists was more constructive but still didn't sit well with me. "At least my way insures that he's alive to stand trial," she insisted.

We tossed around other schemes, but they all had the feel of a *Mission Impossible* script, and they all would take more time than we had. "I'm going with you," I said finally, "as your photographer." Cali called Reggie and sweet-talked him into faxing her Devon's rap sheet and the police report on his relationship with Celia.

We arrived in Lyle, grabbed a quick bite at Brown's, then went to my office and checked Cali's e-mail and mine. Reggie's fax was waiting for us, and we quickly assimilated the details of how Celia Stone had crossed paths with Devon Sheen.

As Celia's sister Melissa had told the story, Devon discovered Celia at a conference in Williamsburg. He believed, incorrectly, that

Celia had money. Only when Celia invited him to visit her home in Byron's Corner did he learn that he'd chosen the wrong mark. Celia's only asset was her DMI stock options. She spent her income freely, invested poorly, and carried debt on several credit cards. Celia came home early one day and found him going through her bank statements. She threw him out and threatened to call the police. Devon hit her, then almost choked her to death, threatening to kill her if she filed a complaint.

Celia did file a complaint and even took a glass from her house to help the police with fingerprinting. Devon, it turned out, was already wanted under multiple warrants. A few weeks later, Devon was arrested for passing a check written against Celia's home equity line of credit. The account had been frozen based on Celia's observation that several unused checks on the equity account were missing. Celia testified at Devon's trial. After the jury convicted him, he made a finger gun and pointed it at her.

"Looks like prison didn't make Devon forget Celia Stone," said Cali.

"Once you get it into your head that someone on the outside is responsible for putting you on the inside, that's pretty much all you think about," I said.

I printed the fax and handed it to her. "What if he won't see us?" asked Cali. "Or won't talk to us?"

"You can't expect him to confess," I said. "All we can hope is that we find something to convince the police to reopen their investigation of Celia's death."

"And how do we do that?"

"After we talk to him, we break into his house and go through all his things," I said. "His mail, his computer if he has one, whatever. If that doesn't work, then I'll call some of my old prison alumni and we'll beat the crap out of him. The cops do it all the time. It's no big deal."

Cali nodded. "I guess I've been around you too long," she said. "That's exactly what I was thinking."

I took Cali to Heartwood House, after which I headed back to the farm. Sleep came quickly but was interrupted by bad dreams that I couldn't remember. I was still feeling irritable when I picked up Cali the next morning.

The drive to Winchester was mercifully short—about an hour or so. Cali had printed a tourist guide to Winchester off the Web and read it to me while I drove.

"I'll bet you didn't know that Winchester was the first settlement and first chartered city west of the Blue Ridge," she said, "and that most of its first settlers were German."

"And I'll bet you didn't know that Patsy Cline once lived in Winchester," I countered.

"I would have if you'd let me read a little more. Let's see. We have some stuff about old roads and something about George Washington. During the Civil War..."

"The War of Northern Aggression," I said wagging my finger.

Cali made a face, then continued. "During the Civil War, Stonewall Jackson and some guy named Sheridan made Winchester their headquarters."

"Sheridan was a Yankee," I said.

"Check that," said Cali. "During the war, Winchester changed hands more than seventy times. We have the Shenandoah Apple Blossom Festival in May, the home of Admiral Richard E. Byrd, Arctic explorer, and—guess what?—the home of country music star Patsy Cline. Not bad for a town of 20,000."

"You forgot to mention that it's also the home of con-artist Devon Sheen," I said.

Cali put down her printout and looked out the window. "That

too," she replied.

We left Route 340 and followed Route 522 to 17. When we reached the city limits, Cali navigated us through a labyrinth of one-way streets to Gray Avenue. After several attempts, we found Avon Avenue, a narrow alley that featured a self-serve laundry, a dry-cleaner, and what looked to me to be an adult video shop.

Devon's apartment was one of several off a second floor landing above the laundry. The windows were open, the sound from several TVs competing for attention. Cali knocked and stepped back.

The door opened a crack, revealing a pair of eyes and a cigarette. Then came the words "Go away," accompanied by a cloud of smoke just before the door slammed shut.

I stepped around Cali and knocked again. Again the door opened, this time halfway. The man behind the door was gaunt and pale, his unkempt hair hanging in long oily clumps over his face, his eyes sallow and unseeing. Reggie's fax had included a photograph of Devon taken at his trial. That handsome and well-conditioned guy only vaguely resembled the man in the doorway.

"You speak English?" said the man behind the door.

"How ya doin', Devon?" I asked.

The sound of his name stunned him for a moment. "I don't know you," he said. "And I don't want to."

"A hundred bucks makes me think you might," I said. "From the looks of things, some cash might come in handy."

"Show me the money," he said, his eyes fluttering.

I held up five twenties. "You let us in, talk to us nice, and you get the money. Act like an asshole and we leave."

He opened the door and ushered us in. "Welcome to Château de Cockroach," he said, snickering.

We stepped inside a single large room, only to be hit by a powerful stench made worse by the stifling heat. I noticed a bathroom off to the left of the entrance and a small stove and refrigerator tucked in the back left corner. A chair and TV occupied the middle of the room. A cot was pushed against the opposite wall. The floor was cluttered with food containers covered with flies. Large chunks of drywall were missing in the ceiling and walls, the holes circumscribed with dark brown stains.

"I think a rat died in the wall," said Devon, reading our faces. "You get used to it. Now, what do I have to do to earn my money?"

"I'm a reporter," said Cali. "I'm working on a story about con men like yourself. Specifically, I'd like to know how you pick your targets, what you do to gain their confidence, and what you plan on doing now that you're out of prison."

"You're a reporter," said Devon. "Who's the man holding the cameras?"

"A photographer," replied Cali.

Devon lit a cigarette and looked at Cali. "That's a bullshit story. Try another."

"What makes you say that?" asked Cali.

"Because no one pays good money to write a story that no one's going to read," answered Devon, "and you don't need photographs to publish it. So stop fucking around and tell me what you want."

I looked at Cali and shrugged. "A few years ago, you hustled Celia Stone," I said. "You called her a few weeks ago. We want to know why."

"That's personal," replied Devon.

"I'm paying for the answer to that question," I responded, "so answer it."

Devon winced, grabbed his side, and leaned forward, obviously in pain. His breathing became labored and he groaned softly. "Shit," he said. "Hand me the pills on the table by the TV."

I picked up a prescription bottle and glanced at the label. Morphine. I tapped out two tablets and handed them to Devon. I didn't need to ask him any more questions. He couldn't be a suspect in the killing of Celia Stone, or anyone else for that matter. Not only was he dying, but his death was not too far off.

"I'm sorry to have bothered you," I said motioning to Cali to leave.

"Wait," he said. "I'll be okay in a minute. I'll pass out in about ten, but I'd like to answer your questions."

He looked up, fear in his eyes. "Pancreatic cancer," he murmured. "Prison doctors found it, and the warden let me out early." Devon looked around the room. "I'd rather have died in prison. At least someone would find me before the rats." He took a deep breath. "That was a good one," he said, referring to the episode of pain. "You wanted to know about Celia Stone."

"I'm sorry," said Cali, her voice tense with frustration. "I can't do this."

She ran from the room and down the stairs. Devon closed his eyes and rolled his head. "My fairy godmother is coming to help me sleep," he said. He took a few deep breaths, then continued. "I called Celia to tell her I was sorry, but she hung up on me. I called her again and left my number. She called me back a few days later and we chatted about what I did and about my current situation. She wasn't as sympathetic as the two of you, not at first. But after awhile she started to talk about herself, about how she'd wasted her life." Devon laughed. "I tried to cheer her up. Fucking A, man. She was really bringing me down. I heard she was killed a few weeks ago. I don't know who did it, but if I knew, I'd tell you straight away."

Devon's head fell forward, then snapped back. "Help me to the bed," he said. "You can leave the money on the TV."

I helped him to his cot, just as he'd asked, and placed the hundred dollars on the TV. I wasn't sure if he'd ever get to spend it.

Cali was waiting for me at the car. "He called Celia to apologize," I said as I approached her. "He said..."

"I don't care," snapped Cali. "No one should have to live like that. No one, not even a con artist who preys on women." I tried to console her, but she backed away. "Don't," she said. "You can't make it better. You can't change what I saw. And you see, that's the point. I know people live in shit, but I can't do anything about it, and neither can you. We're not going to save anyone driving up and down the goddamned highway asking a bunch of questions. By trying, all you're doing is making yourself feel guilty and miserable." She shrugged. "I can't do it any more. I can't deal with all the shit you seem to find. I can't deal with you either."

"Let's go home," I said.

"I'm going home, all right. I'm going back to Chicago, where I belong."

She climbed in the car and slammed the door.

We didn't speak on the way back to Byron's Corner. I dropped her off at Heartwood House and went to my office. I found the number of a hospice in Winchester and told them about Devon. I was assured they would have someone look in on him in the morning. I gave the woman my address and told her to send me the bills. Cali was right. I couldn't save Devon. But thanks to Reilly's money, I could at least let Devon die with a measure of dignity.

My good deed done, I sat and stared at my e-mail inbox, hoping to see something from Gus about Jonathan Freeman or from Harvey about taking on DMI. I hit receive a few times. Getting no new messages, I gave up. In one week, testing would begin on Kikora. Sydney Vail would soon come to trial, the evidence still overwhelmingly against her. We would have the testimony of Dr. Lipton to counter the charge of murder one. Whether the prosecutor would reduce the charges was another matter. If he didn't, the jury could simply disregard Dr. Lipton's testimony. By any measure, Sydney was still in big trouble.

Despite logging several thousand miles on my car in the previous week, I had accomplished very little. With Devon Sheen off the suspect list, all I could do was hope that Gus would find Jonathan Freeman, and that Jonathan would provide some new insight into who killed Celia Stone. Hope, like time, was becoming a very precious commodity.

CHAPTER
TWENTY ONE

The next day was gray and tropical. Low dark clouds dumped torrents of rain, then seemingly moved on, only to regroup an hour later and repeat the process. I spent a good part of Tuesday morning trying to convince Harvey that there was nothing to lose by pursuing discovery against DMI, but Harvey would have none of it. "You just don't know how things work around here. DMI owns everything and everyone in this county. If I do what you're suggesting, the prosecutor won't even talk to me about a deal," he said. "And right now, a deal is the best chance Sydney has of avoiding life in prison."

Just before lunch, Cali came in and sat down. "You still mad at me?" she asked coolly.

"I was never mad at you," I said.

"You should have been. I said some awful things." She looked around my office, but not at me. "I'm going home tomorrow. Frieda's going to fix a big dinner tonight, and I wanted to be sure you'd be there."

"Of course I'll be there," I replied.

"I don't think I'm coming back here," she said. "Ever."

I nodded. "*Ever* is a long time."

Her eyes glistened. "We never talked about us. I was watching *Oprah* the other day and her guest talked about the differences between a friendship and a marriage. A friendship exists because it feels good, not because of any commitment or promise like when you're married. This woman also said that friends come in flavors. Buddies don't share as much as friends, and best friends share everything, even more than married couples do. Do you see what I'm saying?"

I followed the psychobabble but failed to grasp the point. "Maybe, a little," I said.

Tears streamed down Cali's face. "We can't be both best friends and a couple. I can't marry you, although I might have said yes if you'd asked me. It would have been a terrible mistake. What I want to be is best friends. I want you to know I'll be there for you if you need me. I need to know that I can call you, no matter what."

"You didn't have to ask," I replied.

Cali struggled quietly with her feelings, and I did the same. I felt the same sadness that comes from learning someone is dying, but the sadness was tempered with relief. It suddenly became clear that Cali and I had been stuck in time for almost a year. We were now free to pursue our separate lives.

I started to speak, but she shook her head. "I don't want to talk about this any more," she said, then walked out.

I muddled through the day trying to act busy. Cali's pronouncement really depressed me, but I wasn't sure why. As usual, I chose not to think about it much.

I was on the phone with Theo when my cell phone rang. It was Gus.

"We found Freeman. He's at a motel in Herndon, near Dulles Airport. I'm going to pick up Mel around eight. We should be at the motel around nine. And you might want to bring a gun just in case."

I called Heartwood House and told Cali that something had come up and that I couldn't make the dinner. I tried to convince her not to leave until Thursday, but she wasn't going to agree to anything without a better explanation of what was going on. When I told her I was going to meet Jonathan Freeman, she insisted on coming along. I explained that it was too dangerous, and we argued until I revealed my plan to carry a weapon.

"If it's that goddamned dangerous, you shouldn't be going either," she screamed.

"Freeman is the key to understanding what happened to Celia Stone," I said calmly. Cali said nothing. "You told me that you pursued stories for your own reasons," I continued. "I need to pursue the truth of this case. I don't like violence or guns, and I'm not being macho. I'm doing what I've been programmed to do, just like you're doing what you're programmed to do—chase stories."

"You're an attorney," she snapped, "not a detective." Then she hung up.

Maybe I wasn't a detective, but I'd had my fill of powerful people placing themselves above the law. Someone powerful was playing games with Sydney's life, and I was determined to find out who and why.

The Sun Rise Motel in Herndon was located on the edge of a commercial development zone. It consisted of three, single story, ranch-style buildings that probably were constructed in the fifties. Even in the darkness, I could see that the owner, understanding that new development would overtake his property, had decided that maintenance was a waste of his resources. The parking lot was pitted, shutters on some of the rooms were missing or hanging at odd angles, and the windows of two units were boarded over with plywood. All things considered, the Sun Rise looked to be a place that didn't ask a lot of questions of its guests, making it the perfect place to hide. I made a mental note to ask Freeman how he came upon such a place, and to ask Gus how he had managed to find Freeman.

I found Gus and Mel in the parking lot. As I stepped from my car, lightning illuminated the high voltage towers that ran adjacent to the hotel. Instinctively, I counted the seconds between the flash and the rumble of thunder. A cold wind stirred up paper and dust while the motel protested loudly with shrieks of metal sliding against metal.

Gus was leaning against his car. Mel paced a few feet away and puffed nervously on a cigarette.

"What's the plan?" I asked, shouting over the approaching storm.

"Freeman is in the end unit in the last of the buildings," answered Gus. "I'll go to the back window and break it. Freeman should bolt for the front door. When he opens it, Mel will step inside, secure the room and the guest, and invite you in for a visit."

I glanced at Mel, who had started another cigarette. "Is he okay?"

Gus shrugged. "He's never okay, but he does seem a bit more on edge than usual. Maybe it's the storm."

Gus checked his weapon, an automatic, and headed into the shadows. A moment later, he was plainly visible, bathed in blue-white light. Then he disappeared. Mel flicked away his cigarette, reached into his pocket, and pulled out a pair of gloves. I felt a twinge of doubt as he walked toward Freeman's room. I followed him, albeit tentatively. Rain splashed around me, large drops plunking on cars haphazardly at first, then slamming the ground in a sudden deluge. Mel was near the front door when lightning and thunder shattered the night, the bright flash revealing the silencer on Mel's weapon. Then it dawned on me that Mel had different plans for Freeman—plans that didn't include letting Freeman talk to us.

I ran hard toward the door, the rain mixing with hail and stinging my face and arms. Seconds separated me from the door, and yet those seconds, I feared, would be time enough for Mel to empty a clip of bullets into Jonathan Freeman's body and fulfill one of those contracts out on his head.

Through all the noise, I heard what I'd been listening for—the shattering of glass at the back of the building. I was within five feet of Mel when a rectangle of light pierced the rain and darkness. A man stood in the doorway, poised to flee the room. An instant later, I was airborne.

I crashed into Mel just as he raised his weapon to fire. The room lamp exploded in a shower of sparks as the two of us slammed into Jonathan Freeman, driving him back into his room and sending Mel's automatic flying. Freeman rolled free and tried to make it to the door, but Mel grabbed him by the leg and pulled him down. I got to my feet, but Mel, having reached the gun, was now standing with his back to the door. A flash of lightning painted a chilling picture of Mel pointing his weapon at a cowering Freeman. I waited for the thud of the silencer and for my fate. Moments later, the room lit up again, but this time Mel was crumpled on the floor and Gus was standing over him.

"You prick," said Gus, obviously intending his remark for Mel. "Everyone okay?"

Gus shut the door and clicked on a light by the bed. "Is Mel dead?" I asked.

"No," said Gus indifferently, "but he'll have quite a headache. You just can't trust snitches these days. He'll owe me, though."

I shook my head. "You'll use him again?"

Gus went into the bathroom and grabbed a towel. "Sure. He's a snitch. It's his job to betray people, and he's good at it." Gus tossed the towel on Mel's still body. "When he wakes up, he'll understand that he could be dead." Gus turned to Freeman. "So, do you feel like talking, or should I tie you up and leave you for Mel?"

Freeman didn't answer.

"Who wants you dead?" I asked.

Freeman looked straight ahead, saying nothing.

"Actually," offered Gus, "Freeman has become very unpopular. Some of the members of his animal rights group are pretty upset with him because he cut a deal with DMI and ratted out Sydney. DMI isn't happy with him because he decided his silence was worth a lot more money than he originally bargained for. There are two contracts on the street. Maybe it's DMI or his groupie pals, or maybe he's got enemies we don't even know about. Either way, he's a dead man. That is, unless he cooperates with us in exchange for a new identity."

Jonathan said nothing. Gus leaned over Mel and patted him on his cheek. "Wake up. You've got work to do."

"You can get me a new identity?" asked Freeman.

"I can," answered Gus, "but only if you don't bullshit us."

Freeman ran his hand through his long black hair and stood up. He was tall, his cheekbones chiseled, his jaw line covered by a dark beard. He looked at me through blue eyes the Devil would envy. Freeman was born to deal. "Ask away," he said.

"I want to know about Sydney, the chimp, and DMI," I said.

Freeman righted a chair and sat down. He crossed his legs and thought for a moment. Experience tells me that the longer a person takes to answer a question, the more likely the answer is to be untruthful. Freeman seemed to be taking too much time to sort his facts.

"He's screwing with us," I said to Gus. "He's concocting a story to save his ass while we just stand here. I don't want to hear it. Tie up the son-of-a-bitch and let's go home."

"I could shoot him with Mel's gun and we could split the money," suggested Gus. He picked up the broken lamp and pulled the cord from the wall, then cut the wire with a pocketknife.

"What's going on?" demanded Freeman. "I said I'd answer your questions."

"My client doesn't think you're going to be truthful with us," said Gus. "Put your hands behind you."

Mel rolled over on his back and groaned softly. "You'll have company soon," said Gus.

"All right," said Freeman. "No bullshit."

I folded my arms. "Let's hear it."

Freeman nodded. "Sydney learned about this doctor at DMI who had a chimp she was caring for at home."

"Celia Stone," I said.

"Right. Sydney sent Celia an e-mail every day for a few weeks. I wanted to go in and take the chimp, but Sydney got her way—as usual. Anyway, Celia agreed to let Sydney have the chimp, but Sydney thought that DMI might be watching the doctor's house. She had this idea that I should lead a demonstration against DMI as a diversion." Freeman shook his head. "I don't do fucking diversions. I'm the one that the cell members follow, not her. Anyway, after our first rally in Byron's Corner, this white-haired Nazi grabs me off the street and throws me into his car. I was sure he was going to kill me."

"Did he have a name?"

"Collins, I think," answered Freeman.

Mel rolled over and got to his knees. He looked at us, then turned ashen. A moment later he vomited into the towel.

"I think you should keep talking," said Gus.

"So this Collins guy tells me he can get me into a lab and let me bust up some glass and junk," continued Freeman. "He'd film it, put it on TV, and make the group look like a bunch of crazed rockers. I'd get arrested, and then he'd pull some strings and get me a light sentence."

"What did he say he'd pay you?" asked Gus.

"Twenty grand up front, and five grand for each week I spent in jail."

I smiled. "And you believed him?"

"I figured he wouldn't want me talking about how he'd scammed the press," replied Freeman defensively. "Anyway, I did the lab scene just like we planned. He visited me in jail that night and told me that something had come up and the deal was off. The next morning I was assigned this drunk who claimed to be my lawyer."

"Did you tell your attorney about the deal you cut with DMI?" I asked.

Freeman shook his head. "You didn't let me finish. I was going to when the lawyer tells me I'm being charged with murdering the damn doctor. No fucking way I'm taking a fall for Sydney, so I tell my lawyer that I know who did it and that DMI set me up for the lab business. I didn't tell him the details of the deal because I thought it might make me look bad. Anyway, he finds out that I have an alibi for the murder and the next thing you know he's arguing for my release and for a lot of money. Suddenly, it's like I won the lottery."

I let the story sink in, then felt the hairs rise on my arms. I looked at Gus. "Celia Stone's body was discovered the morning after the lab break-in," I said. "But if you believe Jonathan's story, Arthur Collins somehow knew about the murder the night before."

"Jesus," said Gus.

"You figured that out, too," I said to Freeman, "and asked for more money."

"I wasn't asking for much," said Freeman.

Gus laughed. "You pull on a tiger's tail, and it'll bite you." Gus turned to me. "You got what you need?"

I nodded, then headed outside. It was time to do some tail-pulling of my own.

When I left the motel room, it was a little after ten. Light rain was still falling, but the storm had moved on.

Gus told me he'd take care of Mel and Jonathan, and that I should go home and do what I needed to do. The first order of business was making up with Cali, which turned out to be more difficult than I thought. I called Heartwood House from my car. Carrie, who catnaps all day but doesn't sleep at night, answered.

"Hi, Carrie," I said. "I just wanted to let everyone know that I'm okay."

"I'm okay, too," she said.

"Could you let Cali know?"

"She's asleep," answered Carrie. "And I'm sure she thinks you're okay without being told."

I wasn't sure how to penetrate Carrie's logic. "Tell her that Freeman had lots to say."

"Like what?" Without the slightest pleasantry, Cali had joined the conversation and posed the question. "How long have you been on the line?" I asked.

"I answered the phone, dear," answered Carrie. "I'm going to hang up now and let you talk to Cali yourself."

I summarized my conversation with Jonathan, leaving out the details of Mel's attempt to cash in on the contracts on Jonathan's life. If Cali was still angry with me, it was masked by her excitement.

"This changes everything," she said, "even though I don't understand how or why DMI would be involved in Celia's death." A moment passed. "You can say I told you so once, but only if you say it within the next ten seconds."

"We have more to do before I get to the I-told-you-so's," I said confidently. "I'll set up a meeting with Harvey and Theo in Byron's

Corner for tomorrow morning. Then we'll sit down with DMI's attorney and talk about discovery motions and the like."

"You can pick me up around 8:00—7:30 if you want coffee," she said, and hung up.

I spoke with Harvey and Theo, stowed my phone, and headed for home. Tomorrow was going to be one hell of an interesting day.

CHAPTER
TWENTY TWO

The drive home to Lyle should have taken an hour. The debris and accidents left behind by the storm made it a tedious three-hour trip. I didn't get to bed until three and had to be up the next morning before 7:00.

At 7:30, I picked up Cali and headed to Java Java. At 8:00, we were fully caffeinated and sorting through scenarios that we hoped would tie together the facts in a way that was favorable to Sydney. While the effort helped pass the time, the most important result of the exercise was to underscore how much of the story of Celia Stone's murder remained unknown.

Harvey had convinced Jeff Miller, DMI's general counsel, to meet us at the DMI headquarters at 1:00 that afternoon. From Harvey's description, Jeff wasn't keen on meeting, even if it meant avoiding subpoenas and nasty legal proceedings. Jeff had apparently planned on attending a legal conference at a golf resort in Vermont and was seriously put out by the timing of our request. The meeting was set only after Jeff called back, presumably after getting orders from his superiors.

I pulled into DMI's driveway and parked in front of the main building. I saw Harvey's car and a Mercedes with an Albemarle County inspection sticker. We stopped at the reception desk, where I signed in Cali as co-counsel.

"How does it feel to be a lawyer?" I asked her as I clipped on my visitor badge.

"Like I've done something I don't want my parents to know about," she said.

A few minutes later, a guard appeared, escorted us to the elevator, rode with us to the eighth floor, and led us down a long, wide corridor. Massive artworks adorned dark wood-paneled walls, making me wonder if the DMI stockholders knew how management had been spending their money. We passed through a security door that opened to a suite of offices. The guard led us into a corner office. In contrast to the dark corridor, the room was flooded with sunlight from windows that extended from floor to ceiling, and that ran the length of both exterior walls. Instead of boorish art, these walls were covered with photographs of animals, mostly babies interacting with their mothers.

I was so engrossed in the photographs that for a moment I failed to notice Jeff Miles, Harvey, and Theo sitting at a large table. Jeff's eyes were fixed on Cali.

"Hey, Jeff," I said. "Shep Harrington. We met at the hearing. This is Cali McBride. She works with me in Lyle."

I looked around the room. "You like animals?"

"I took those pictures in Africa," he said proudly.

"So what do you think about testing on chimpanzees?"

Jeff feigned a smile, but not well enough to hide his annoyance. "My respect for animals is limited only by my desire for finding ways to reduce the suffering of my fellow man."

"Very noble," I said. "We have indeed suffered enough without a good anti-obesity pill."

Cali and I took our seats at the table. Jeff sat at the head of the table, his arms folded. A speakerphone sat in the middle of the table, the speaker-button light illuminated.

"I must say for the record that I find the late night phone call and the demand for a meeting both arrogant and offensive," said Jeff. "Threatening litigation is not a way to garner cooperation. With that said, you can state your reasons for being here and what it is you want."

All eyes turned toward me. "First, let me say that we're as sad as you must be over the death of Celia Stone. You knew her?"

"Not really," said Jeff defensively.

"Then we can discuss her murder objectively," I responded. "That's good, because the facts of the case are confusing."

"Excuse me," said Jeff, "but why are we talking about her murder at all?"

I feigned surprise. "Because Sydney Vail didn't kill Stone," I said, "which means that someone else did. I have reason to believe that someone at DMI has information about the crime that will not only exculpate Ms. Vail, but may lead us to the real killer. You do want to know who killed Dr. Stone, don't you?"

Jeff stood up. "I'm not going to play this game with you, Mr. Harrington. This meeting is over."

Harvey opened his briefcase. "Just a moment," he barked. "I plan on filing these tomorrow. I want lab records, videotapes, security logs—stuff like that. I will also depose all of the security staff to see who might have threatened Jonathan Freeman. I want records pertaining to Celia Stone, what you knew about her state of mind and when you knew it, and who might have broken into the offices of a Dr. Frank Lipton. I also want to know how DMI learned of her death on July 24 and why it wasn't reported to the police until the following morning."

I looked at Jeff. "You'll see that we want to depose all of the researchers, the Chief Executive Officer, and the Chairman of the Board. That is, unless you talk to the prosecutor and explain that Sydney Vail didn't kill Celia Stone and didn't steal Kikora."

Jeff glared at us but said nothing.

"How about it, Jeff?" I said. "You want to finger the real killer? Remember, you're probably an accessory to obstruction of justice. I suspect you violated a few ethical rules along the way and could be disbarred. I've been incarcerated and disbarred, and I'm certain you won't like either."

"You don't really think you'll find a judge within a hundred miles of Byron's Corner who'll grant those motions?" said Jeff.

"I'll get back to you on that," I replied. "Theo, would you show Mr. Miller what you've been working on?"

Theo handed me a stack of papers a half-inch thick. "Shep asked me to look into the question of whether primates, and chimpanzees in particular, were entitled to protection under the Constitution. I was skeptical at first, but I believe under a series of modern cases, the issue could be ripe for consideration. What you have before you is a motion for a temporary restraining order to stop testing on the chimpanzees housed at this facility and a motion for habeas corpus to have the chimps turned over to a guardian while their rights are decided. In addition, I have a suit for damages based on the denial of the chimps' civil rights in the amount of one billion dollars."

"Before you blow-off these filings," I said, walking a copy over to Jeff, "I suggest you consider all the implications to your business once the media picks up on the litigation and the general way chimpanzees are treated in facilities like this one."

Before Jeff could respond, Howard Doring burst into the room, charging straight for us. He swept papers from the table with his cane, then poked me with the tip. "You goddamned son-of-a-bitch!" he screamed, his face red with rage. "No one fucks with me, especially here. You take your bullshit legal documents and your bullshit legal-speak and get the hell out of here!"

Doring trembled with pent-up adrenaline, his knuckles white against the silver figurine adorning the top of his cane. He seemed poised to strike, but the moment ended when a gray-headed man stepped between us.

"Get a hold of yourself," he said to Doring. He turned and studied me for a moment. "Arthur Collins," he said offering me his hand. "I'm the head of security here at DMI."

"Throw him out," demanded Doring.

Arthur glowered at Doring, who seemed to recoil from the look. Arthur then turned to me. "While I find your allegations libelous and in poor taste, I wish to extend my apologies for Mr. Doring's outburst. The death of Celia Stone shocked all of us at DMI, Mr. Doring in particular."

"Sydney Vail is not guilty," I said calmly. "I'm going to do everything in my power to prove it."

"I would strongly suggest that you mind your own business, Mr. Harrington," replied Arthur, "but that's free advice, not a threat."

"Sydney Vail's life is of no consequence," said Doring. "And neither is yours."

"Shut up, Howard," barked Arthur. He looked at Jeff. "Call them an escort, and get Howard out of here."

Arthur turned and looked at me. He seemed to be assessing

my qualities as an adversary. "Which is more important to you?" he asked. "Your client's well-being or learning the truth?" Before I could answer, a smile teased the corners of his mouth. "Think about that for a while, Mr. Harrington. Then we'll have a little chat."

Cali, Harvey, Theo, and I stepped out of the DMI headquarters building into the steamy August air. My three companions exchanged impressions of the meeting in general, and Howard Doring in particular. But my thoughts were on Arthur Collins' question—why he asked it and what my answer would be.

CHAPTER
TWENTY THREE

A visit with Harvey isn't complete without at least one meal at a fine local restaurant of his choosing. That afternoon we went back to the Country Kitchen for a late lunch. To Harvey's delight, they had what he called the "better-than-sex" cake on the menu.

Over lunch, we agreed that tomorrow Harvey would file the discovery motions with the local criminal court and Theo would file a Temporary Restraining Order in Federal District Court. Harvey agreed to tell Sydney of the new developments, and that I hadn't given up on saving Kikora from DMI.

We were waiting on dessert when my cell phone rang. It was Arthur Collins. "There's an abandoned quarry a few miles from town. Harvey can tell you where it is. Twenty minutes. Come alone."

I spent ten minutes arguing with my cohorts about whether I was walking into a trap, whether I was suicidal, and whether I needed to have my head examined. I calmed their fears by agreeing to call immediately after arriving at the quarry and at fifteen-minute intervals thereafter. Harvey called Reggie and found him in his office, where he said he'd remain for the next hour. As I headed for my car, I left Harvey trying to explain to Reggie why his whereabouts were important.

Twenty minutes later, I pulled off onto a gravel road and drove slowly through the parking lot. A single car was parked at the far end, and I pulled in next to it. Before I'd shut the engine off, Arthur Collins tapped on the window. "Let's take a walk," he said. I made a quick call, then joined Arthur Collins.

We followed a dirt path to a rocky outcropping littered with beer cans and what appeared to be condoms. Twenty feet below, sheer rock walls encircled a lake of dark, impenetrable water. "A few fools dive in without considering how to get out," said Arthur. "The water is cold, fed from underground springs. People die because they didn't think ahead." He looked at me. "You can't win this fight," he said, his voice cold, impersonal. "I hope you're intelligent enough to know that. The only point at issue is how much, and that's up to you."

"Okay," I replied. "You win."

Arthur ignored me. "Power, Mr. Harrington, is more than money. You have money, but you have no power because you aren't willing to exercise it without reservation. You may claim the moral high ground, but you don't have the will or the means to challenge people like me and Howard Doring."

"I'll fight you in court," I said, sounding childish even to myself.

"You can throw paper at me," he replied, "but I'm capable of killing everything and everyone you love, without hesitation or remorse. You can't defend yourself from that."

I grabbed Arthur's shirt and pushed him toward the edge of the rocks. Three men suddenly appeared from behind me. "You don't even have a gun," said Arthur. "And you wouldn't shoot me if you did. I, on the other hand, will kill you, without hesitation, if the need arises."

I released him, then turned to leave. "You haven't heard what I'm willing to offer you, or more to the point, Sydney Vail." When I kept walking, he said, "I'll even let you have the chimp."

I turned around, dumbfounded. "You lost me," I said.

"The prosecutor will cut a deal with Sydney," answered Arthur. "She will serve less than three years, but she will never publicly deny she killed Celia Stone. You can take Kikora home tonight, but you will purchase her, acknowledging that she is property that has no rights of any kind. And you will tell your friend, Theo, not to file for a temporary restraining order and motion for habeas corpus. If he has already filed, he'll withdraw his pleadings." Arthur walked a little closer to me. "People like Howard Doring have power but don't understand how to use it. They want to fight, when their very power allows them not to. You seek the truth, something I can't allow you to have. You can still try to discover it, but the price of failure will be the life of Sydney Vail and the chimp. Are you so arrogant that you would let them pay such a high price to satisfy your sense of injustice? I think not. I'm only going to make this offer once. I'll need your answer this evening."

I watched Arthur walk away. I searched for a rejoinder, some clever remark that might raise a scintilla of concern in Arthur's mind, but the effort was fruitless.

I stared at the mirrored surface of the quarry. From twenty feet away, it looked inviting, a cool respite to August's furnace-like heat. But the water was a death trap. As Arthur had said, a person could get in but not out. I had learned the hard way that principles were equally alluring. When I was accused of criminal fraud, I believed in my innocence, that my innocence would protect me from accusations that I had knowingly cheated the government out of monies owed it. My defense counsel urged me to consider a plea bargain, but I wouldn't listen. I never considered the possibility that witnesses would lie or that prosecutors would withhold exculpatory evidence. I couldn't admit to being guilty when I wasn't. I couldn't admit to a lie, but neither could I see that others, who felt no such constraint, surrounded me.

My visceral reaction to Arthur's offer was to tell him to go fuck himself. But the reality was that Arthur held the trump cards and had played them deftly. Arthur was going to win because he had shifted the burden of proof to Sydney. Her only hope was to prove that she *didn't* kill Celia Stone. Without that proof, Sydney would lose. Arthur knew it. I knew it. Harvey knew it, too. Sydney was still facing a murder charge, a possible life sentence. I had gambled with a lot less at stake and lost. I wasn't prepared to let Sydney make the same mistake.

I rejoined Harvey, Cali, and Theo at the restaurant. Their collective concern for my well-being had given way to a collective gloom, based, I surmised, on my demeanor on the phone and the expression on my face. I sat down and poured myself a cup of coffee.

"So what did Arthur want?" demanded Harvey.

"My soul," I said. "I think he wants my soul."

When I finished explaining the deal, no one spoke for what seemed like the longest time. I ate a piece of cake while the others chewed on Arthur's offer. Finally, Harvey cleared his throat. "The decision, of course, is up to Sydney. I personally find the arrogance of Mr. Collins to be beyond words. But as Sydney's attorney, I'm inclined to advise her to take the deal if it's offered."

Cali patted my hand. "Three or four days ago, if I told you we'd have Kikora back and Sydney looking at a sentence under five years, you'd have been ecstatic. Don't let your ego blind you from how successful your efforts have been."

Theo nodded. "We'll have another day to fight for the rights of primates. You have to put the interests of your clients ahead of your personal desire for truth and fair play. I know that's a bitter pill to swallow, but that's the role we lawyers play."

I stared into my coffee, then finished it. I said nothing more, my energy consumed by a thought that scrolled through my head over and over: *Arthur Collins killed Celia Stone, and he's going to get away with it.*

Later that evening, the deal was agreed to. Sydney was submissive, weeping as she thanked Harvey for saving Kikora. I called Heartwood House and told Frieda to turn on the air conditioner in the bunkhouse because Kikora was coming back to us. A cheer went up as the news spread from Frieda to the residents. In the background, I could hear Carrie talking about a party. I understood their joy, but they didn't know the price that had been paid for Kikora's safety and freedom. I saw no reason to explain things to them. I then called Jerome and left him a message that I needed to talk to him about a permanent sanctuary for Kikora.

At 9:00, we set off for Lyle with a heavily medicated Kikora sleeping in the backseat. When we'd reached the interstate, Cali leaned over and gave me a kiss on the cheek.

"What was that for?" I asked.

"To remind you how special you are," she said. "After all, we *are* best friends."

I smiled but didn't feel worthy. All I could think about was how Sydney would spend three years of her life in a small cell for a crime committed by the man who had set Kikora free.

CHAPTER
TWENTY FOUR

It took Kikora a few days to readjust to the poor farm. By Friday, she was back to her old antics and playing with her toys and dolls.

Sydney's arraignment was scheduled for the following Monday, at which time she would enter a plea of guilty to involuntary manslaughter and receive a ten-year sentence, with seven years suspended.

I went back to work, primarily to avoid the residents who were planning a party for Sunday. Kikora's return and my thirty-third birthday, it seems, were sufficient reasons to ask the entire town over to the poor farm for a get-together. Cali invited all the people who she knew had helped me with Sydney's case, which included Jerome but not Heather, and Gus but not Mel. Harvey declined the invitation, choosing to stay in Byron's Corner in case Sydney needed him for anything. "Enjoy your party," he said. "I'll take care of Sydney. We can talk Monday after the hearing."

I seemed to vacillate between being relieved and feeling like I'd missed something obvious. On Thursday afternoon, I was sitting on the patio at Heartwood House, digging myself into and out of a funk. Rocky, a twenty-pound Siamese cat with chocolate paws and ears, joined me at the table. He eyed me, made a trumpeting sound, and flopped over so I could scratch his belly. I indulged him, as I pictured Sydney lying on her bunk, staring at her concrete and steel cage. Then I recalled the pounding of the judge's gavel—the one that had sent *me* to prison. In less than forty-eight hours, Sydney was going to be judged a killer, and there was *nothing* I could do to stop it.

Cali sat down, looked at me, and read my thoughts. "You can't do any more than you've done," she said.

"I missed something," I said angrily. "I just can't put my finger on it. It sucks!"

"Much of life sucks," she agreed, "so we have to concentrate on the parts of life that don't. We're going to have a party, and you need to be in the right frame of mind to enjoy it. Brooding is a waste of time, especially when you have a lot of people depending on you to be cheery and appreciative."

Cali was beginning to sound like Frieda, a prospect that didn't improve my disposition.

"And why must I be cheery and appreciative?"

Cali rolled her eyes. "It's your birthday, silly," she said. "You knew that. Right?"

"Tell me the party is for Kikora and not for me," I replied.

"Never mind," said Cali, springing from her chair and walking away.

Carrie was the one who pulled me from my funk. She appeared on the patio outside of the sunroom carrying a tray with two bottles of beer and a bowl of peanuts. "I thought you might like something cold to drink," she said.

"Thanks, Carrie. But I'm not sure I can drink two beers."

"Well, of course not," she replied. "One of them is for me."

I watched her take a quick sip. "I haven't had a cold beer in twenty years," she said. "I always enjoyed the first sip the most." She smiled at me. "You go on making yourself feel bad," she said, "and just ignore me."

"And what exactly do you mean by that?"

Carrie took another sip of beer. "Oh, you know, how you look at what you failed to do instead of what you tried to do and what you managed to accomplish. You've always been that way."

"You don't get medals for good intentions," I said, tossing a peanut in the air and catching it in my mouth.

"Well, then maybe you should. I'm as proud of you as I can be," she said, patting my hand. "I know your mother would be and so would Reilly. You took on an impossible task. Most people wouldn't have cared enough to do anything. But you can feel like a failure if you want."

I tapped my bottle against Carrie's. "Thank you," I said.

She put the bottle on the tray. I could see that she'd consumed less than an ounce. "Any more of that and I'll be drunk," she chuckled and went back inside.

I drank both beers and ate all the peanuts. I was a new man.

I was on my way to the office when Cali called. "I don't have anything to wear to the party," she said. "I have to go to Front Royal to get a new outfit. We can take your car."

We returned in the early evening and went directly to Heartwood House. Cali had purchased three outfits, none of which satisfied her. My opinion was solicited, then ignored. I suspect that being asked was a formality of some kind, and that my response, even before I gave it, was irrelevant. Cali modeled her new clothes for Carrie and Frieda, consensus was reached, and a major fashion crisis was averted.

We spent Saturday cleaning the poor farm and entertaining Kikora. We made and hid popcorn. She found most of it, then hooted for more. I watched to see if she was signing as she searched, but she seemed to have gone mute.

Sunday arrived bright, cloudless, and inexplicably early. Cali arrived at the farm with the sun, opening doors, scurrying around, and making as much noise as possible. I sat up in bed and watched her comings and goings. Finally, she stopped and glared at me.

"What are you doing?" she demanded to know.

The question implied that I should be doing something other than lying in bed. "That's a hard one," I said. "How about a hint?"

"Try 'getting ready,'" she said.

The party was to start at four, but Cali was already feeling rushed. "I *am* getting ready," I said. "I'm rehearsing small talk. Like, 'Well, prison can be like that,' and 'I knew a few guys who escaped, but they were shot.' I want it to sound sincere."

"I'm serious."

I showered and dressed in twenty minutes. Cali advised me that it was too early to put out food or drinks, and that Frieda and Carrie were going to decorate the tables. My services were not needed.

I changed Kikora's diaper, fed her, and took her for a walk to the meadow. We played in the high grass, as we had weeks earlier, but this time without fear of the future. I knew that Kikora would be leaving again, but this time to start a life with other chimpanzees, some of whom, like her, had been cross-fostered, then abandoned. I was going to find her the best sanctuary available and throw as much money at it as I could afford. Kikora would never live in the wild again, but neither would she face torture and suffering at the hands of humans.

The guests seemed to arrive *en masse* and on cue. The invitations had made it clear that gifts were not required, but almost every arriving guest was carrying a package of some kind. Doc and Billy refused to comply with Frieda's instructions to leave their gift on the porch, insisting that I open theirs immediately. A war of words ensued. I intervened and opened a poorly wrapped bowling ball and bag. "It's time you had a real good hook ball," said Billy.

"Your name is on it," said Doc.

A long number followed the word "Shep".

"That was your prisoner number," said Billy.

"A gift of love," I said, and thanked them both.

Parties have a definite beginning and a definite ending. The beginning is marked by the formalities of greeting the guests, which include the "how-have-you-been" questions, and comments about clothes, weather, or sport teams. I received happy birthday hugs from the ladies, and back slaps from the guys. Kikora, who put on a simpering act that earned her cookies and cheese, fascinated people.

What happens in the middle of a party is unpredictable, depending on who is invited and whether anyone shows up with an agenda.

The end comes when the host or hostess signals that it's time for everyone but the trusted inner circle of friends to go home. You can tell a party's over when the host and the circle members begin gossiping about the departed guests.

At a good party, people form groups, those groups dissolve, and new ones form. The grouping-regrouping process creates currents that keep the guests in constant motion. I decided to float on the current and go where it took me.

I spent a few minutes with Ken Johnson, the broker who managed the various stock investments I'd inherited from Reilly. We were talking about strategies and various companies he was watching, when the conversation suddenly shifted to DMI. "What do you think of DMI?" he asked. "I mean, as an investment? The diet drug is going to make them a lot of money and…"

I cut him off with a stern look. "I don't want you to invest a dime in that company. You hear me? Not one fucking dime!"

He stared at me, his face flush with embarrassment. "I think I get the point," he said sheepishly.

"Sorry," I replied. "I didn't mean to jump on you. I'll explain it to you some other time."

"I think I'll get another beer," said Ken, walking away.

I saw Cali waving at me from across the lawn and beckoning me to join her. When I arrived, she was staring at Heather, who was talking to Doc and Billy.

"Who's that?" asked Cali, a slight slur in her words.

"Her? I think her name is Heather Reinhardt. Jerome—the primate expert at the zoo—is her father. I believe Heather is a behavioral psychologist."

Furrows crossed Cali's forehead. "Didn't you have dinner with Jerome?"

"You're right," I said. "That's where I met her."

"I remember that you seemed to have a lot of information about chimpanzee behavior after that dinner," said Cali suspiciously. "She's kind of slinky looking."

Heather was wearing a halter-top that made an "X" across her chest, revealing a hint of breast on the top, bottom, and sides. Doc seemed so smitten I was wondering if his heart could handle the excitement. "Maybe she's doing research on male behavior," I said.

"I tried on that very outfit and thought it in bad taste," said Cali, finishing her wine. "She's coming this way. Perhaps you're her next research subject."

I introduced the two women. "So you're Cali," said Heather. "I read your story about Reilly and Shep. Very interesting."

"I'm glad you liked it," said Cali.

Heather looked at me. "I understand you made tapes of Kikora while she was playing alone," she said. "I'd like to see them if it's not too much trouble."

The question seemed innocent enough, but it struck a chord in my memory. I struggled unsuccessfully to understand why. "Sure," I said. "I'll get Harry to set it up for you."

"Actually," said Cali, "Harry has been showing those tapes to guests for the last hour."

"Well, then," I replied, "follow me."

I led Heather inside and found a small group crowding around a television set and watching Kikora playing with her dolls. Ken Johnson was there. "I didn't immediately understand why you took such a hard position on buying DMI stock," said Ken. "But Harry told me what's been going on, and about your chimp. I think I now understand where you're coming from."

I thought about objecting to the reference to "your chimp," but I let it go. Ken was a broker. He couldn't be expected to know any better.

"Hey, Shep," said Harry. "We're getting near the end. Want me to start over?"

"No. That's okay." I watched for a minute or so when Harry said to me, "Here's the night you stayed with her."

An image of Kikora looking at a magazine flashed on the screen. I explained to the guest that Kikora was signing at the pictures. Suddenly, Kikora was jumping up and down on the magazine.

"Something really got her upset," offered Cali.

"A picture of Howard Doring," I said, remembering Kikora's last night at the farm.

"Let's see the video again where Kikora is playing with her dolls," said a guest.

The moment of recognition was like a lightning bolt in my head. "No!" I snapped. "Let it run."

"Shep?" asked Cali. "You okay?"

"We have another view from a different camera," said Harry. "You recorded both."

Harry took the remote, and two pictures appeared on the screen. One showed Kikora jumping up and down. The other clearly showed the magazine opened to a picture of Howard Doring.

I grabbed the remote and rewound the tape. "Doring said he'd never seen Kikora before. So then why would Kikora get so agitated seeing his picture?" I rewound both tapes, returning to the point where she first saw the picture of Doring. She was signing something.

"She could be reacting to his face or to something in the picture," offered Heather.

I turned to Harry. "Find Carrie. Now."

"What's happening?" asked Cali.

"Remember I said I had missed something obvious?" I replied. "Now I know what it was. Kikora witnessed the murder of Celia Stone. She was under the couch, but she could peer out if she wanted to. Originally, I thought Arthur Collins killed Stone, but Kikora knows better. This videotape is her deposition." A moment later, Carrie showed up with Harry. "Watch the tape and tell me what Kikora is signing," I said.

Carrie watched the tape. "It's very simple, dear. Here she's signing 'hurt white coat' and 'hurt stick'. I think she's pointing to Mr. Doring's cane."

I watched the tape of Kikora retrieving her toy baseball bat and hitting the magazine with it—an eye-for-an-eye, chimpanzee style. I watched the tape several times.

Cali clung to my elbow. "Howard Doring killed Celia Stone," she said softly.

"Jesus," said Ken. "The COB killed his own lead scientist?"

I nodded in agreement. "Now the question is whether the truth makes any difference."

CHAPTER
TWENTY FIVE

I called Harvey at his home and his office, leaving messages at both locations. I then called Detective Reggie Mason. I told the dispatcher it was an emergency and to have Reggie call me on my cell phone. "Tell him I have a gun and plan on shooting someone."

I was rewinding the tapes when Frieda appeared and announced that everyone was waiting for me to cut the cake. I shrugged. "Great."

"Are you going to blow out the candles, or should I?" she asked.

I took the tapes and followed her outside to the porch. The cake was on a table in the front. I stood by the table, holding the tapes in one hand and my cell phone in the other. Frieda, lighting the candles, called for the guests to assemble. A smattering of voices began to sing "Happy Birthday." Everyone caught up and sang together, although the musical key remained elusive. Then my phone rang.

I could barely hear Reggie. "I have enough evidence to get a search warrant," I said.

"I can't hear you," said Reggie.

"A search warrant," I yelled. Just as the singing stopped, I blurted out, "a goddamned search warrant."

The crowd looked at me, clearly stunned at my shouted profanity. "One second," I said, holding up my finger. "Reggie, I have a tape of Kikora signing to a picture of Howard Doring. Doring hit

Celia Stone with his cane. We've got to get a warrant to test his cane for blood."

"The candles," said Frieda.

"Hang on, Reggie," I said, extinguishing the flames in one quick blow and enduring a burst of cheers and applause.

"I don't know, Shep. I can't sign a probable cause affidavit based on a tape if I haven't seen it, and, besides, I'm not sure I can rely on the testimony of a chimp."

"Can't or won't?" I responded. "I'll talk to Harvey and Sydney. If they're in agreement, I'll show you the tape and you can decide. You'll need someone who knows sign language." Reggie didn't speak for a moment. "This is Sydney's last chance to avoid prison," I said, almost pleading.

"Okay," said Reggie finally. "Call me when you decide what to do, and I'll look at your tape, but I'm not promising anything."

I looked at my watch. "I have to go," I said to Cali.

The guests stared at me, uncertain what to do. Carrie stepped forward. "Shep has to leave to solve a murder. Everyone can stay as long as they want."

Another smattering of applause rose from the gathering, and I ran from the room. Cali caught me at my car. "I don't want you to go," she said.

"I'm just going to talk to Sydney and show these tapes to Reggie," I said. "What could happen?"

"Arthur Collins isn't going to let you implicate Howard Doring," she said.

I kissed her. "Arthur won't know if you don't tell him."

I briefed Harvey on the tapes. "I'm sure I can convince Reggie to request a warrant based on the tapes," I said without justification, "but you and I both know we'll be violating the deal I cut with Arthur Collins. If we pursue the search warrant for Doring's cane and find nothing, Sydney is facing life."

I heard Harvey breathing, but for the longest time he didn't speak. "I know what I will advise her to do," he said softly, "but the decision is hers. I'll have to pull some strings to get a late night visit at the jail, but I think I can manage it. You should be the one to explain the situation to her."

I tried to think of something to say, but everything that needed saying had already been said. I agreed to meet Harvey at the jail.

I arrived in Byron's Corner a little over three hours later. How I managed to avoid a speeding ticket was a mystery—or perhaps an omen of good things to come. Harvey was waiting for me outside. "We have fifteen minutes," he said. "Do you have the tapes?"

I patted my pocket.

"I would never have suspected that Howard Doring killed Celia," said Harvey. "Never."

"Doring doesn't take kindly to betrayal," I replied. "You saw his temper at the meeting the other day, and at the hearing at the farm. Celia must have said something that set him off. The grip of his cane is an intricately carved lion's head made of silver. In the hands of a strong man, it can be a deadly weapon."

Sydney was waiting for us in an interrogation cell, worry dominating her face. "What's happening?" she said. "Is Kikora okay?"

"She's fine," I said. "We had a party for her."

Sydney's face softened. "I heard." She pursed her lips. "I owe you a lot, starting with an apology."

"You don't, but we can discuss that later," I said. "We have only a few minutes, and you have to make a decision that could have a profound impact on your life." I explained what I'd seen on the tapes.

"Assuming that Reggie will certify to a magistrate that there's probable cause for a warrant, they will seize the cane and check it for tissue and hair. If they find some, they will then have to test it to see if it matches DNA from Celia Stone. If it matches, Doring will be arrested and you will go free. If there's no tissue or if it doesn't match, then your deal with the prosecutor could be withdrawn, and you'll be tried for second-degree murder or voluntary manslaughter. I suspect you'll be convicted of the lesser charge and face a long prison term without parole."

"Lots of ifs," said Harvey. "As your attorney, I don't recommend this course of action. The risk is too high, and you've got a better deal than we could have expected under the circumstances."

Sydney nodded, then stared at the manacles attached to her wrists. "What happens to Kikora?"

"The purchase agreement I signed stipulates that the sale can be rescinded if you reject the plea bargain you've been offered," I replied.

"But if Doring is the killer and we find his DNA," said Sydney, "he won't be around to torture other chimpanzees." She laughed. "It would be an irony if he were locked up in a cell for the rest of his life, wouldn't it?"

A guard appeared. "Time's up," he said.

"I need an answer," I said. "I'm not trying to make you decide one way or the other. It's not *my* life."

The guard helped Sydney to her feet. "Get the warrant," she said. "Let's give the bastard a taste of his own medicine."

"God forgive us if we're wrong," said Harvey.

We left the jail and entered the parking lot. "Let's go find Reggie," I said, heading to my car. "I'll drive."

I heard a gasp, turned, and saw Harvey slumped against the side of my car, blood trickling down the side of his head.

"You don't listen," said Arthur, now waving a gun at me. "Get him in the car."

Arthur opened the back door and I pushed Harvey inside. "Don't do anything stupid, or I'll shoot him."

I slipped into the driver's seat and pulled on my seatbelt. Arthur sat next to me and braced himself against the passenger door, his gun pointed at me. "Head south until I tell you to turn," commanded Arthur. "Oh, and I'd like the tapes."

I took the tapes from my pocket and tossed them to him. "Just how do you know about the videos?" I asked.

"Guards aren't expensive," he replied. "I've heard pretty much everything Sydney has said. This is the communication age after all."

"What now?" asked Harvey, his voice thick with pain and fear.

"Shep is going to drive us to the quarry," answered Arthur.

"Just in case you're wondering, I don't want to die," said Harvey.

"I'm not keen on the idea, either," I said. "You've got to appreciate that killing us won't change anything. We have copies of the tapes. We have people who saw them."

"But you won't have Howard's cane," replied Arthur.

A few minutes passed in which no one spoke. Then Arthur asked, "You ever throw a rock at a hornet's nest? Kids always think if they stand far enough back, they can hit the nest without getting stung. What kids don't appreciate is that hornets will defend their domain swiftly and with concerted effort." Arthur tapped me on the shoulder with the barrel of his gun. "You would have been better served if your childhood had included that lesson."

The situation I found myself in was not unfamiliar. I had witnessed it a hundred times in movies. I used to wonder why the victim, instead of trying something—even something futile—simply accepted the fate that awaited him. Now, I was in the same situation, and the impediment to action was hope. Rather than take a fatal step, I clung to the hope that the situation would resolve itself. In reality, the closer we got to the quarry, the closer I was to the end of my life, and most certainly to Harvey's, too. Hope wasn't going to save either of us.

I had no weapon. I thought about searching for a pen or pencil, but except for the soft glow of the instrument panel and the faint, dusky moonlight that seeped through the windows, the car was dark. I heard Harvey breathing heavily in the backseat, no doubt measuring his remaining time in miles and in minutes. Then I thought of the pocketknife on my key chain. It was small, the blade less than two inches long. But it was something.

I moved a hand from the wheel, but Arthur leaned over and pressed the barrel of his gun against my head. "You're thinking, Mr. Harrington, but you shouldn't be. Keep your eyes on the road."

As Arthur moved back against the door, I noticed a red light on the dashboard issuing a command to "Fasten Seatbelt". I looked at the light for a moment, then at Arthur.

"So why did Doring kill Celia Stone?" I asked.

Arthur laughed. "I asked him. He doesn't remember hitting her. All he remembers is that she was saying crazy things."

"Like what?" I asked, trying to sound fully absorbed in the discussion.

"She told Howard he was an idiot, that his success was due to luck and the people who worked for him."

"Not something Doring wanted to hear," I said.

"It wasn't what she said," corrected Arthur. "Howard couldn't get her to stop screaming at him. Howard loved Celia, and here she was ranting insanely. Howard's solution to everything he can't control is to lose control himself."

"I don't mean to sound tacky," I said, "but it seems odd under these circumstances for you to be criticizing Howard."

"If you think I'm being impulsive, Mr. Harrington, I'm offended," replied Arthur. "It comes down to money. Tomorrow, at a DMI press conference, we'll announce the start of tests on the new diet drug. A few weeks from now, we'll leak to the press that our preliminary tests have been successful, and our stock price will soar. I'll be a wealthy man, free of Howard Doring and this ungodly place. Eliminating the two of you is a rational act designed to ensure that the events I just described will unfold without the risk that you might foment some public scandal that could distract investors."

As Arthur spoke, I saw what I was looking for. Just at the edge of my headlights, the road curved sharply through a small stand of trees. "You okay, Harvey?" I asked.

"Not really," he replied.

Arthur turned to look at him. I looked to the side of the road, found a large locust tree, and steered toward it. The driver's side airbag was ten years old. I hoped it was in working order.

The next few seconds unfolded in slow motion. The right side of the car found the shoulder of the road, dipped slightly, then rose up. Arthur turned the gun in my direction. I heard it fire at the moment my airbag slammed into my face and chest, stealing my breath from me. In an instant, the sounds of ripping metal and shattering glass overwhelmed my senses. For a moment, I was engulfed in silence, which was quickly replaced by a constant hum punctuated by the pounding of my heart. I felt just one thing—that the world was spinning out of control.

I was conscious, but only within a narrow field of perception. I realized I could breathe, only every breath brought searing pain. I could move my hands, but my right arm was unresponsive. The car, I determined, had rolled onto the driver's side, pressing me against the door. I tried to right myself, but my legs were caught and I couldn't pull them free.

I heard a groan from the backseat.

"Harvey? You okay?" He didn't answer.

I looked at the seat where Arthur had been sitting. In the moonlight, all I could see were shades of gray. Shadows and objects blended into shapes that were difficult to parse. But after staring for a moment, I concluded that Arthur wasn't there. I saw a shoe on the dashboard, then noticed a large hole in the windshield surrounded by a larger dark circle. My momentum had been stopped by an airbag and a seatbelt. With no seatbelt or airbag, Arthur had been launched through the windshield, although I couldn't imagine how a man his size could fit through the small opening in the glass.

A moment later, I realized that the shoe on the dashboard was not empty. The outline of a leg disappeared into the darkness of the footwell. Apparently, Arthur had not left the car in one piece.

A voice came out of the darkness. "Help me. Please help me."

I tried again to pull my legs free, then gave up. I searched my pockets and located my cell phone and called Reggie.

"Where are you?" he asked, clearly annoyed.

"I took a small detour on Valley Road," I said. "Better send an ambulance. Harvey's hurt. I think I've been shot, but I'm not sure. At the moment, I can't get out of the car, and I smell gasoline."

"Hang on," replied Reggie, trying to sound calm.

An eternity seemed to pass before I heard his voice again. "Do you have the tapes?"

I fought through a fog that was separating me from my senses. "The tapes are in Arthur Collins' pocket."

"Arthur?" pressed Reggie. "Where is he?"

"Look around the car, up in the trees, wherever," I answered haltingly. "But maybe we don't need them."

"What did you say?" asked Reggie.

They were the last words I heard him speak. Then, the fog enveloped me.

I heard voices and saw a white light. This was how the movies depicted the transition from life to death. I thought the light was supposed to feel compelling, but I found it made my head pound. Suddenly, the light disappeared and Reggie's face filled my field of view.

"If you're God, then the whole world is going to be very disappointed," I said.

"You're a mess," he said. "You've got to go with the medics."

The medic regarded me with impatience. "You've got a bad contusion on your chest and a dislocated shoulder. A bullet grazed your shoulder and the back of your head. You could have a concussion and a bruised heart."

"How's Harvey?" I asked.

"We're still collecting the man who was ejected," said the medic. "The man in the back seat may have internal injuries. He's fifty-fifty."

I swung my feet off the gurney and righted myself. "We have to talk."

"I've got the tapes," Reggie volunteered. "Where do you think you're going?"

I looked at him and tried to answer. Reggie disappeared in a hailstorm of bright lights and pain.

When my senses started to function again, I realized I was in a hospital. That I knew my whereabouts without opening my eyes seemed odd, except when I started to remember snippets of disembodied conversations about my condition, about a doctor and a nurse who were saving money on motels by using an operating room, and about a possible nurses' strike.

Again, I was hearing voices, calling my name, ordering me to wake up. Finally, I willed my eyes open. They fluttered, closed, and stayed closed for some time. The voices encouraged me to try again, and this time the lights came on all the way, and I was staring at Cali and Gus.

"We got a warrant," said Cali.

For a moment, I couldn't relate this simple statement to anything. "The search warrant," said Gus. He looked at me. "My God, what did they give you?" he said.

A nurse arrived. "Excuse me," she said in an official nurse's voice. "Who are you and what are you doing here?"

"These are my parents," I said. "They are coming to take me home."

The nurse seemed confused, trying, I suspect, to figure out how Cali (my age) and Gus (nearly sixty) could qualify as Mom and Dad. "You're not going anywhere," said the nurse.

"DMI is going to announce this morning at a press conference that testing will begin this afternoon on their new diet drug. That's when Reggie's going to serve the warrant and take the cane," said Cali.

"I wanted to tell Reggie that Collins told me that Doring killed Celia Stone," I said. "We don't need the tapes to establish probable cause."

Gus shrugged. "It's too late for that now."

"Harvey's going to be okay," said Gus, anticipating my question.

"I'm going to have to ask you to leave," said the nurse.

"Since you've asked so nicely," I replied, "I think I should accommodate you."

I sat up, then waited for my head to stop spinning.

"Not you," barked the nurse. "Them."

I looked at the nurse. "Of course, silly. I'm going with them. I'm going to a press conference."

"You sure?" asked Cali.

I wasn't, but I pretended to be. "Get me my clothes."

The nurse scurried out while Cali and Gus helped me dress. As we were about to leave, a doctor arrived, the smug-looking nurse standing a few steps behind him. "You're in no shape to be leaving," said the doctor.

I studied the doctor for a moment. I thought I might meet the stud who was shanking nurses in the OR, but the man before me looked to be in his fifties and more into patients than nurses. "Do you sometimes think that life is unfair to the good guys, that the bad guys get away with all kinds of crap?" I said. "And if you had a chance to see one of those arrogant assholes get his, someone who just about got away with murder, wouldn't you do anything to be there when the hammer came down on him?"

The doctor stared at me, my questions resonating in some distant corner of his memory.

"He's delusional," said the nurse.

The doctor chuckled softly, then said, "Yes, Mr. Harrington. I think I know exactly what you're saying. I won't permanently check you out. Consider this a day pass. If you feel any sudden chest pain, nausea, or double vision, I want you to return here immediately."

The nurse pouted for a moment, then left.

"Thanks," I said to the doctor, and headed out the door.

The press conference was held in front of DMI headquarters. Once Cali showed her press pass, we were waved into the parking lot. I saw Reggie wearing civilian clothes near the podium. Howard Doring was chatting with a small group of people, his cane thankfully in hand.

"Why doesn't Reggie serve the warrant now?" I asked.

"He could," said Gus, "but he has the discretion to do so anytime he wants."

"Reggie believes it would be best to wait until the cameras are rolling and Howard Doring is speaking," said Cali. "Howard might say something stupid, not to mention entertaining," she added gleefully.

At 11:00 sharp, a woman stepped to the microphone. "Before we get started, I would like to note that Arthur Collins, the security director at DMI, was killed last night in a car accident. He will be missed by everyone who knew him." She spoke in somber tones, then looked away for a moment of dramatic effect.

When she faced the audience again, Arthur had been forgotten. "Today is a momentous day at DMI," she said with a lilt in her voice. "This afternoon, we begin the last of a series of studies on a new drug that will revolutionize the world. Safe and effective, Caldefy will offer hope to those individuals that suffer from obesity and those who are unable to control their weight. I'm pleased to present to you Howard Doring, our Chairman of the Board."

Howard reached the microphone about the same time Reggie did. "Excuse me," said Reggie, handing Howard the warrant. "I need to ask you to surrender your cane."

Reggie reached for the cane, but Howard stepped back. "You have no right," he said.

"I am empowered by this search warrant to seize the cane," said Reggie calmly.

"Why do you want the cane?" shouted a reporter. A chorus of questions erupted from the crowd.

I smiled at Cali. "Your brethren smell blood. Let's get to the front of the line."

"I will arrest you," said Reggie, "if you resist further."

Two uniformed policemen approached Howard from behind as he raised his cane. "You son-of-a-bitch!" he screamed.

Two officers grabbed Howard as Reggie grabbed the cane. The assembled media sharks promptly went on the attack. Cameras flashed, questions were shouted, and cell phones chirped as speed dials were activated. DMI security moved to keep the crowd from rushing the podium, leaving me directly in front of Howard. Until he saw me, he seemed bewildered. Then a smile spread across his face, a knowing, arrogant, defiant smile. Howard had murdered Celia Stone. He knew it. I knew it. The silver lion's head that adorned the top of Howard's cane had crushed her skull. Intricately carved with deep holes and crevices, the lion's head held the key to freeing Sydney Vail.

I looked Howard in the eye. "How well did you clean your cane, Mr. Doring? Did you just wipe it off? Will a lab tech find a small piece of Celia Stone's remains in some little crack? Think about it. Forty-eight hours from now, you could be where Sydney Vail is sitting."

"You haven't won anything, Harrington," said Howard. "I'll have a hundred lawyers challenging anything a police lab finds. Testing of our new drug will start this afternoon, and I'll see to it that the chimp you call Kikora will be back here in a week."

"I don't think so," said Reggie. "I have an order identifying Kikora as a material witness in the murder of Celia Stone and granting protective custody of Kikora to Shep Harrington."

A reporter who had evaded security thrust a microphone into Howard's face. "What is the connection between you and Celia Stone?" she asked. Other reporters appeared and the siege was on.

I slipped away from the throng and sat on a bench under a large shade tree. Fifteen minutes later, Cali arrived. "We won," she said.

I shook my head. "We won a skirmish," I said. "Howard will fight the search. Chimps are still considered property. This case will keep a hundred lawyers busy for years."

Gus arrived and helped me to my feet. My shoulder ached, my head pounded, it hurt to breathe, and my day-pass had expired. But I hadn't felt this good in weeks.

EPILOGUE

To my great relief, traces of tissue *were* found in the intricate carving of Howard Doring's cane. DNA testing confirmed that the tissue belonged to Celia Stone. Based on this evidence, Sydney Vail was released from prison and all charges against her dropped. Howard Doring, after being indicted on murder charges, was released without bond.

Two months after the search warrant was issued, the Honorable Tazewell Minor, a Virginia District judge, ruled that the search warrant had violated Howard's rights under the Fourth Amendment to the Constitution. The law is clear that evidence obtained illegally cannot be used against the person whose rights are violated. The judge suppressed the DNA evidence that was the single link between Howard Doring and the murder of Dr. Stone. Howard Doring thus became a free man again.

In his written opinion, Judge Tazewell ruled that Kikora's testimony was not admissible in court because it was not credible and because it could not be stated with certainty that she comprehended the meaning of the signs she was making. The judge wrote:

> I can find no court opinion anywhere that holds as a matter of law or scientific fact that a chimpanzee has the mental capacity to communicate reliable factual evidence. Even if there were such opinions, this court finds that the videotape evidence provided in support of the warrant at issue is subject to a multitude of interpretations and as such cannot support a finding of probable cause. This animal's conduct is not a clear and unambiguous statement as to what she observed and when, nor was she trained to make such observations. There is no credible evidence that this animal was making a rational connection

between what we are told she observed weeks earlier and the photograph she is said to have observed at a later time. The tapes merely show an animal responding to some unknown stimuli in a manner that can be easily interpreted as imitation of something the animal has observed elsewhere or as random, meaningless behavior. Further, we do not have to reach the arguments regarding the chain of custody of the tape-recorded evidence, although we believe them meritorious. Suffice it to say that this court cannot allow the Constitutional rights of one of its citizens to be violated based on some vague interpretation of a chimpanzee's gestures. I also find that the Commonwealth's attempt to justify the warrant based on evidence produced after the issuance of the warrant was insufficient and late.

I spoke with Judge McKenna after the ruling. "Tazewell is sixty-five going on a hundred," he said. "He takes the Bible literally and applies it to all kinds of cases. The most we can do is pray for his early and continued retirement."

The case is on appeal to the Virginia Supreme Court. Ironically, the Attorney General's Office, which had once argued so strenuously in support of the eugenics laws that allowed hospitals to sterilize any Virginian determined to be "unfit," was now urging the courts to recognize the cognitive capacity of chimpanzees. Theo, meantime, had filed an amicus brief on behalf of all chimpanzees.

Though Howard Doring got away with murder, he lost both his company and his fortune. The press conference footage didn't sit well with investors or with DMI's board of directors. The board fired Howard and brought in consultants to determine what to do with the company. In the meantime, the company, at the board's behest, agreed to sell me the remaining chimps.

In the days following the news conference, investors dumped huge amounts of DMI stock, sending the price tumbling to less than a dime a share. Ken Johnson, my broker, begged me to purchase a large—but legally insignificant—block of DMI stock because he was convinced that the company was fundamentally sound, and its stock price would rise again in the near future when others recognized that fact. I agreed, and gave him the go-ahead.

Meantime, DMI's outside strategic consultants suggested to the board that the anti-obesity drug be evaluated using an experimental computer model that emulated liver function in humans. Interestingly, the first set of results from the computer model proved so promising that the stock took off. I made a nice return on my investment, the bulk of which I used to send the liberated chimps to a chimp sanctuary program.

Kikora stayed with me for a few months. Carrie spent the last few weeks showing Kikora pictures of sanctuaries and conversing about other chimps. When the day came for Kikora to leave, joyful tears flowed freely. Carrie accompanied Kikora to a sanctuary in Florida outside Jacksonville. The reports from the sanctuary are that Kikora was adopted by an older female and is doing fine. She is teaching ASL to two of her new family members.

My injuries are almost healed, although I'll need a few more months of physical therapy to strengthen my shoulder. Cali is back with Bradley and writing the last of her series of articles on primates, testing, and the legal system. Before she left, I tried to convince her that I was going to focus on being a lawyer. "To be honest," I told her, "I think my days of meddling are over." When she didn't respond, I added, "Really. I mean it."

She nuzzled me, kissed me on my cheek, neck, and forehead, and brought her lips to my ear.

"Liar," she whispered.

AFTERWORD

In Chapter 10, Shep Harrington, this novel's central character and this mystery series' recurring protagonist, has the following exchange with fellow lawyer Harvey Raimer:

> I heard Harvey exhale slowly. "You have a lot of guts," he said.
>
> "No, Harvey, I don't," I replied. "Lots of people have been fighting to protect primates for years. I'm just in this one specific situation, trying to make it come out right. I'm afraid to go to prison, but afraid to live with myself if I don't do something to help this chimpanzee. When I say it out loud, it sounds crazy even to me."

Shep understands that believing in a cause is not the same thing as dedicating your life to that cause, and so do I. Following this Afterword is a short bibliography of books and links I used as references in writing this novel. To stay true to the mystery genre, I was compelled to choose my facts and issues carefully. If you want to know more about chimpanzees and about the dedicated people who have championed the rights of primates, check out these references, surf the Web, ask questions, and get involved, even if that involves giving this book to friends, relatives, and colleagues who are non-believers.

It isn't too late to save our closest genetic relative.

PRAISE FOR
CHAIN THINKING

"When a writer attempts to introduce a social issue into his fiction, he can almost be sure that he will be accused of some kind of proselytizing. In *Chain Thinking* the issue is animal rights and the fiction is the story of Kikora, a chimpanzee, and Shep Harrington, a lawyer and detective *manqué*, and his battle not only to solve a murder, but to save the chimp from experimentation. Elliott Light has managed to weave these two parts together, and do it seamlessly."

—Martha Grimes, Best-selling writer of more than 20 mysteries, Noted animal rights advocate, and Winner of the Nero Wolfe Award (best mystery)

"Those who think that stories about legal rights for nonhuman animals have to be boring, tedious, complicated, or abstract are in for a treat. In *Chain Thinking*, the plain truths about our inhumanity to other beings with whom we share our world are told in a way both exciting and funny. What animal rights lawyer wouldn't want to be like Shep Harrington (except for the part about going to jail)? And I guessed wrong about whodunnit!"

—Steven M. Wise, Lecturer, Harvard Law School, and author of the books *Rattling the Cage: Toward Legal Rights for Animals* and *Drawing the Line: The Case for Animal Rights*

"*Chain Thinking* is two books in one. On the one hand, it's a wonderful introduction to the plight of captive chimpanzees. On the other hand, it's an engrossing murder mystery that's hard to put down. Both elements are packed into a quick and thoroughly enjoyable read."

—Roger Fouts, Co-author of *Next of Kin, My Conversations With Chimpazees*, and Deborah Fouts, Director, Chimpanzee and Human Communication Institute, Central Washington University

"In *Chain Thinking*, a follow-on mystery to the meaty and fascinating, *Lonesome Song,* Elliott Light proves that he is not a one-book wonder, and indeed has improved with age. The topical, ripped-from-the-headlines theme of whether humans should exploit our closest biological relatives—chimpanzees—for bio-medical research raises immense ethical questions without the usual politically correct claptrap. Regardless of how you feel about the issue, this is a thoughtful and well-written read."

**—Lewis Perdue, Author of the acclaimed
mystery-thriller *Daughter of God***

"The more Shep Harrington (small town lawyer-turned-detective) meddles in the affairs of a self-interested biotech COB and a murdered star scientist, the more intriguing things become. At stake are life sentences for an accused animal rights activist and a group of laboratory primates that are supporting what might be considered less than essential medical research. *Chain Thinking* is both an enter-taining read and an invitation to seriously consider how we conduct our affairs with our closest genetic relatives."

**—Robert A. Holt, PhD, Head of Sequencing, Canada's
Michael Smith Genome Science Centre, BC Cancer Agency**

"In *Chain Thinking*, Shep Harrington, the lawyer turned amateur sleuth, struggles to find out the truth behind an impenetrable cover-up, and of the animal rights crusader set up to take the blame for the much ballyhooed murder of a promi-nent pharmaceutical researcher. And while his story greatly entertains us, *Chain Thinking* also lays out—in simple, understandable terms—the legal and ethical issues surrounding human exploitation of our next of kin—chimpanzees. You don't have to be an animal rights advocate to enjoy this engrossing mystery. But after you turn the final page, you'll definitely have something important to think and talk about."

—Mary Lee Jensvold, Ph.D., Chimpanzee & Human Communication Institute (CHCI), Central Washington University

"*Chain Thinking* is a superior read! Setting a fascinating, under-examined moral and political issue within the context of a gripping mystery, it gives you much more to consider than whodunnit? In the tradition of *Lonesome Song*, Shep Harrington has returned in a real page turner!"

**—Andrew Light, Manager, Customer Service
and Training, Syncra Systems, Inc.**

"I just finished *Chain Thinking* today. I am not a purely objective observer when it comes to the issue of using chimpanzees for biomedical testing. Even so, I was caught up in the story. The Dr. Doring character made my skin crawl. And I kept wishing that Shep and Heather would get together—maybe in a sequel. But as one who is dedicated to the cause of captive chimps, I want to thank author Elliott Light so very much for writing this novel. He is an answer to my prayers; I have always felt that a good novel dealing with the subject of primate experimentation is necessary to bring this issue to the general public. Let's hope that millions read *Chain Thinking*."

—Lynn Pauley, Founder, Primate Freedom Project

"This second of Elliott Light's Smalltown Mysteries was even better than the first, and I thoroughly enjoyed the debut. The legal issues posed by Shep Harrington and chimp Kikora in *Chain Thinking* caused me to think hard and long about our legal system—how it deals with the truth, and what the basis of that truth may be."

—Jon L. Roberts, J.D., Ph.D.

"*Chain Thinking* is a great read! Light not only weaves an entertaining yarn, but teaches us something along the way about us, our next of kin, and how we might do better to expand our thinking beyond the immediate protection and benefit of our own species. Light clearly did his research on the current status of chimpanzees in the biomedical and legal worlds, and it shows. Bravo!"

**—Liz Clancy Lyons, Special Projects Director,
Doris Day Animal League**

"I found *Chain Thinking* charming and inspiring. In *Chain Thinking,* Shep Harrington further demonstrates the ability of one person to make a difference in our world, in this case by effecting change in the lives of animals. For those of us involved in the daily work of saving animals, *Chain Thinking* serves as a wonderful affirmation. For those not yet involved, I hope, an engaging open door."

—Tammy Sneath Grimes, Founder,
Dogs Deserve Better: No Chains!

"Elliott Light writes with an elegance that most of us can only manage by quoting others. Luckily, I'm a lot funnier than he is, or I'd have to give up this whole mystery novel thing and take up upholstery. I hadn't read his previous Shep Harrington novel, but now I'll have to go back and start from the beginning. Elliott, you've gained a fan."

—Jeffrey Cohen, Author of *For Whom The Minivan Rolls*
and *A Farewell to Legs,* the sequel

"Shep Harrington, the lawyer hero of Elliott Light's first book, *Lonesome Song*, is conned into solving the murder of an unlikeable scientist in order to save an animal rights person from jail or worse. He holds no brief for either the victim or the accused. Yet, because he is a man of conscience and an ex-jail bird with a cynical regard for prosecutors, he insists on finding out what really happened and why. In his search for the truth, he plows ahead with indomitable persistence, savvy, a little bit of luck, and help from a signing chimpanzee. Light is a clever writer who has a droll sense of humor, considerable knowledge and insight into the social scene, and an uncanny ability to deal with the nuances and motivations of individuals from different walks of life. This book is, indeed, a worthy successor to his first book, and I suspect we will be reading about Shep Harrington for a long time to come. Incidentally, animal rights people will love this book."

—Ed Dager, Professor Emeritus (Sociology), University of Maryland

"*Chain Thinking* is a worthy successor to the first Shep Harrington SmallTown Mystery, *Lonesome Song.* The book has everything a series reader could want: a fascinating, plot driven whodunit; a familiar small town setting with a familiar cast of local characters; and a host of new characters. The book strikes a perfect balance between Shep's quest to find a murderer and the book's central theme—the plight of a chimpanzee named Kikora who faces certain death as a biomedical test subject. If *Chain Thinking* is any indication of where this series is headed, I can't wait for the next one and the next one and.........."

—Katy Caselli, Reader

"If you like murder mysteries, you'll love *Chain Thinking*. The book draws on current scientific knowledge about the minds of chimpanzees to weave a compelling story about murder, power, and the mistreatment of our closest genetic relative. I quickly found myself rooting for an ex-con, an accused murderer, and a chimpanzee named Kikora. But more than just an entertaining story, the reality depicted in *Chain Thinking* is both compelling and disturbing. Like *Uncle Tom's Cabin*, *Chain Thinking* is fiction that shocks the conscience. It is nothing less than a must read."

—Rick Bogle, Founder, Primate Freedom Project

"As an admirer of Elliott Light's first novel, *Lonesome Song*, I looked forward to reading Shep Harrington's next adventure, *Chain Thinking*. I expected it to be good, and I was not disappointed. Beyond the quick pace and neatly wrapped-up ending, I also had an unexpected and delightful experience—I learned something. The treatment of primates in captivity that is one of the book's central issues compelled me to wrestle with moral questions I hadn't previously considered. This is entertainment and then some!"

—Arlen Wilson, Counselor, U.S. Department of State (ret)

"Imagine opening your front door to an unusual woman who knows you're a lawyer and demands help. With some persuasion, you agree and find yourself charged with the care of a baby chimpanzee, obviously stolen. So begins *Chain Thinking*, the second Shep Harrington SmallTown mystery. When Shep eventually learns that the scientist who cared for Kikora the chimp has been murdered, Shep find himself in the middle of not only this murder mystery but a battle to save Kikora as well. When books have an agenda, there's usually a point in the story where the agenda takes over and the story becomes secondary. Fortunately, this is not the case with *Chain Thinking*. The animal rights aspect blends effortlessly as an aspect of this novel, an important part, but not the whole. The murder mystery is front and center and Light delivers the mysterious goods!"

—Elizabeth Baldwin, Buyer, Mysterious Galaxy Books (San Diego, CA)

ACKNOWLEDGEMENTS

Acknowledging people who provided time, support, and criticism is a frightening undertaking. Good intentions can be easily undone by an accidental omission. I hope I have extended my appreciation personally to my friends and family members who endured me during the writing and marketing of *Chain Thinking*. If I haven't, I certainly will with a little nudge or gentle reminder.

Mary Lee Jensvold, Ph. D., of the Chimpanzee & Human Communication Institute (CHCI), Central Washington University, read the very first draft of *Chain Thinking* (under a different title) and offered both criticism and support. Based on her comments, I knew I was on the right track. Roger and Deborah Fouts and Steven Wise not only lent their support but the motivation to see the book to its end.

I owe a special thank-you to Rick Bogle and Lynn Pauli, cofounders of the Primate Freedom Project. We have never met. (I think they live somewhere at the end of the Internet.) Rick provided critical comments and a glimpse into the politics of the so-called Chimp Act. Lynn not only read and critiqued an early draft of *Chain Thinking*, she breathed life into my network, helping to find other reviewers who would lend their name to my project. She answered every e-mail, every plea for help. Thank you, Lynn, for all your help.

To all of you, my heartfelt appreciation.

Elliott Light
Rockville, MD
August 2003

BIBLIOGRAPHY AND LINKS

In writing *Chain Thinking*, I relied on these two books:

Roger Fouts and Stephen Tukel Mills,
Next of Kin, My Conversations With Chimpanzees
(Avon Books, Inc., 1998)

Steven M. Wise,
Rattling the Cage: Toward Legal Rights for Animals
(Perseus Publishing, 2000)

WEB LINKS OF INTEREST

Friends of Washoe http://www.friendsofwashoe.org
Chimpanzee and Human Communication Institute
http://www.cwu.edu/~cwuchci
The Animal League Defense Fund http://www.aldf.org
The Arcus Great Ape Fund http://www.arcusfoundation.org
The Center for Captive Chimpanzee Care
http://www.savethechimps.org
The Great Ape Project
http://www.envirolink.org/orgs/gap/gaphome.html
Jane Goodall Institute http://www.janegoodall.org
The Ark Trust http://www.arktrust.org
The AESOP Project http://www.aesop-project.org
Psychologists for the Ethical Treatment of Animals
http://www.psyeta.org
Primate Freedom Project http://www.primatefreedom.com
The Doris Day Animal League http://www.ddal.org